To my parents

CW00864465

THE DRAGON HOARD

"I am Prince Jasleth," said the prince, as soon as he could get a word in edgeways.

Everybody round the table burst into peals of laughter. The princess, King August's daughter, laughed harder than anyone else.

"I will forgive your presumption," gasped King August, "because there's nothing I like better than a good laugh." He wiped his eyes. "Now. I suppose you've come about cleaning the cellars."

"I've come," said Prince Jasleth, "to seek my fortune."

CONTENTS

Part One.   The Birthday Presents   page

1. In which Princess Goodness becomes too
    good to be true   13
2. In which Prince Jasleth sets out to seek his
    fortune, and wishes he hadn't   28
3. In which Prince Fearless receives an
    enchanted sign   45

Part Two.   The Quest

4. In which the magic log sends the ship in
    the wrong direction, and Jasleth eats a
    stone bun   61
5. In which Awful is told a long, long story   76
6. In which Maligna sprinkles Sea-Wickedness,
    and *The Quest* goes to the sea-bottom   94

Part Three.   The Nasty Tasks

7. In which Princess Jadelli has a visitor,
    Prince Jasleth tames two fierce horses, and
    the palace pool goes into a jug   107
8. In which Jasleth asks for a golden orange   123
9. In which the Dragon Hoard is finally
    won – Hurrah!   137

Part Four.   Final Magic

10. In which Jasleth comes home, and
    Maligna gets a present   153

The Dragon Hoard

PART ONE
The Birthday Presents

CHAPTER ONE

In which Princess Goodness becomes too good to be true

The kingdom of King Minus lay at the back door of six or seven very tall, very blue mountains, looking out over the sea, which was very blue as well. All the houses were built on the sides of the slope, and looked as if they only needed to lose their balance slightly to fall off into the water. There were woods and orchards and lots of sheep and goats, who always seemed to be grazing around the palace whenever King Minus decided to have a procession. The sheep and goats sometimes decided to have a procession too, and then they would go straight in through the back door, up the stairs and into the banqueting hall, bleating their heads off.

The palace was built of white stone, with white pillars and a golden roof, and was rather handsome, except where the marble floors were covered with scores of little muddy sheep footprints, and the pillars had dents where the goats had playfully butted them. Up at the top of the palace several owls and storks flapped about and fell over each other's nests. They were very old, at least they said they were. Anyway, they could all remember, at least they all *said* they could remember, when Prince Jasleth and Princess Goodness had been born.

The prince and princess had grown up by now, Jasleth into a handsome young man with black hair and blue eyes, and Goodness into a beautiful girl with hair just the colour of summer sunlight. In fact they were exactly the sort of son and daughter any king and queen would want. At least they were until their seventeenth birthday.

King Minus had decided to hold a great feast to celebrate the birthday. The banqueting hall was laid out with the best of everything, and gold plate besides, and the kitchens were bursting with wonderful food. The storks and owls, who had been leaning out of their nests all day to see what was going on, had quite lost count of all the sides of beef, and sacks of potatoes and strawberries and melons, and crates of ice-cream, that had been pushed, pulled and rolled in through the door.

"There goes another layer of birthday cake!" shrilled a very young owl, getting over excited. "What does it say? Hap-py-birth-day-Goo-"

"Hush, dear," said the little owl's mother, who had noticed that the bats, who hung from the dark roofs of the attics, had all woken up, and were glaring.

"I must say," remarked one bat to its friend, "if somebody sent me a cake saying: 'Happy birthday, goo,' I should be most annoyed."

In her bedroom, which had real pearl walls, and a swansdown carpet, Princess Goodness was arranging her golden crown, and admiring her party dress, which was gold as well. She was also deciding which jewels to put on.

"I think you're overdoing it a bit, dear," said the princess's cat, as Goodness added her third necklace.

"Oh, do you?" asked Goodness, surprised. "Well, I suppose perhaps I am," she added, looking at her ten brooches, twelve bracelets, and deciding, no, she couldn't possibly put on two crowns at once, unfortunately.

"It's getting so many presents," said Goodness.

"Hmm," said the cat, who was a rather plump tabby. "But if you're going to wear all your presents, you'll have to put on your new bed cover, and your paintbox, and your four other dresses as well."

Downstairs, Jasleth had just returned from galloping for miles on his new chestnut horse, and had ridden into the royal stables.

"That was wonderful," said Jasleth. "Thank you."

"Don't mention it," said the horse. "I knew your father would give me something nice for my birthday, and a light, considerate rider like you is just what I've always wanted."

While all this was going on, and the cooks were putting thirty-four candles on the birthday cake, and the sheep and goats were trying to decide whether or not to run up the stairs, or if they should wait until the guests had arrived, and run up then, and really make a mess of everything, a very nasty event was just about to happen.

On the other side of the sea, half-way up an enormous mountain which was covered in dark green woods, lived a thoroughly unpleasant enchantress called Maligna. Maligna, unfortunately, was slightly related to King Minus. She was a fifth cousin, or a fourth aunt, or something like that, and, although everybody else in King Minus' family was extremely

nice, Maligna was not. She was just the sort of enchantress you'd expect, with a long black dress, and
lots of long black hair which had about six bats tangled
up in it. Her palace – she had a palace, but it wasn't
really a very pretty one – was all black, too, and
looked crooked. If you knocked on the door to ask the
way, or for a drink of water, a very black toad would

pop through a peep-hole in the wall, and call you names. It wasn't at all the sort of place to visit if you could help it. The postman always left Maligna's letters – whenever she got one, which was about once every three years – on a tree stump at the bottom of the mountain. You couldn't really blame him. Maligna kept two wolves instead of dogs, and she had trained them both to chase the milkman, the postman, and anyone else they thought it might be nice to chase, and bite them hard when they caught them. Maligna would lean out of the window and clap whenever anyone got bitten.

This afternoon, Maligna was busily making a poison-ivy trifle in her very untidy kitchen, when she heard a lot of growling and snarling and howling and yelping.

"What luck!" cried Maligna. "A new postman!"

She hurried to the nearest window, and, sure enough, there were Sweetie and Poppet, the two wolves, chasing the postman down the mountain at top speed. Outside on the crooked palace porch was a single letter.

"At last," said Maligna. "My invitation to Jasleth's and Goodness' birthday feast."

It wasn't, however. It was a bill from Winged-Serpent Chariot Hire.

Maligna was furious. Nobody ever asked her to their birthday feasts, which was hardly surprising.

"My own fifth cousin, or fourth nephew!" she shrieked. "How *dare* he not ask me! *I'll* show him!"

So saying, she stamped up the mountain to the big black cave where Winged-Serpent Chariot Hire was.

"Get me a chariot and six winged serpents at once!" shouted Maligna.

A rather sleepy old monster, who had been sitting out in a deckchair in the sun, went inside and came back with a large black book.

"I'm afraid, madam," said the monster reproachfully, "you haven't yet paid for the last one."

"Never mind that," snapped Maligna. "I'm in a hurry."

"But madam, I cannot possibly let you have a chariot unless – "

"One winged chariot, and six winged serpents, at once," shrilled Maligna, "or I'll turn you into a human being."

The monster quailed.

"Oh, very well," it muttered, and went to conjure one up.

Maligna sat outside in the deckchair, and told the bats in her hair all the nasty things she would do to King Minus, and what a horrible birthday feast it was going to be, ha, ha. Every minute or so she would scream:

"Hurry UP!" at the top of her voice, and the woods would tremble.

Eventually the old monster came out again, leading an enormous chariot with six hissing, spitting serpents attached at the front. The chariot was black and gold, with wheels spurting blue fire, and the reins were thick with rhinestones. As for the serpents, they were a matching team, all a kind of sickly green with fiery crests and black forked tongues. Instead of saying "How marvellous!" as any normal enchantress would have done, Maligna sneered.

"Well, I don't think much of that old tumble-down cart – and how mangy all these serpents are. You'd think they'd bother to give their scales a proper polish before sending them."

She got in and cracked the whip over the serpents' backs, letting them know what sort of afternoon they could expect.

"Ta ta," she added, and took off in a couple of flashes of lightning, knocking both the deckchair and the old monster flat.

"This is the life!" screamed Maligna, roaring over the woods and meadows of various kingdoms, and frightening most of the inhabitants into hysterics. "Giddy-up, you lazy half-wits! And don't keep on hissing. One can't hear oneself think."

When she went over the sea, Maligna made the serpents spit fire at the ships, but fortunately they missed every time. She also leaned out and yelled at the mermaids sitting on the pink coral reefs:

"Pah! Sitting there all day, just combing your hair! I *never* comb my hair. Waste of time."

The mermaids screamed, and dived back into their lagoons.

Maligna laughed merrily, and lashed the serpents ten or eleven times harder for good luck.

Meanwhile, back in King Minus' palace, the head cook was just putting the last cherries on the last trifles, while down in the banqueting hall the guests had arrived, and were happily looking at all the nice things to eat, and saying "My word! Wasn't it only yesterday that Jasleth and Goodness were only two?" Below, you could hear the first patter of little hooves at the bottom of the royal stairway, as the sheep and goats got ready to run up. Once the prince and princess appeared in the doorway, they were hugged and kissed, and all the usual sorts of things. In fact, it was everything a birthday feast should be, when, all of a sudden –

CRASH! BOOM! BANG! CRASH!

In through the largest window, shooting off blue flames and claps of thunder, rode awful Aunt (or Cousin) Maligna and her serpents and her chariot, and drew up right on top of the birthday cake.

"Ha!" screamed Maligna. "Just in time for tea!"

All the guests began to make excuses about having to get home quickly, the head cook burst into tears, and the sheep and goats, who had just got to the middle of the staircase, ran hastily down again, and back into the orchard.

"I've come," said Maligna, gracefully getting out of the cake, scattering raisins and icing sugar all over the place, "to wish dear Jasleth and dear Goodness a very happy birthday feast. So forgetful of you not to ask me."

"Welcome," said King Minus coldly.

"Oh come now," laughed Maligna, changing a couple of trifles into porridge. "Of course I'm not."

"And as you're here," continued King Minus, "sit down and have some – er – cake."

"Sit down? I wouldn't dream of it until I've given dear Jasleth and Goodness their birthday presents," and Maligna glided towards the prince and princess with what she obviously thought to be a kindly smile. Goodness gave a scream and hid behind Jasleth. Jasleth began trying to persuade the King's secretary to stand in front of him. The King's secretary refused.

"Oh, this must be dear Jasleth," crooned Maligna, and all the bats flapped around in her black hair.

"Oh, no," said Jasleth brightly, "I'm not Jasleth – "

"Come now," coaxed Maligna, "of course you are; you're wearing Jasleth's crown."

Jasleth took off his crown and passed it to the secretary, who hastily dropped it in the blanc-mange.

"Now, now! Naughty boy!" gaily teased Maligna.

"Excuse me," said Jasleth, "but aren't all those bats rather heavy to carry around? Have you tried moths, they'd be much lighter – "

"Moths!" yelled Maligna.

"Or chickens, perhaps, if you don't mind the heaviness. They could lay eggs for you. You'd always be ready for breakfast, if you see what I mean."

"Breakfast!" screamed Maligna.

"Or an eagle," added Jasleth, trying to be help-ful. "Only one mouth to feed, and a sort of built-in umbrella if it started to rain."

Maligna gave a shriek, and changed all the pillars in the hall into large tree-trunks.

"Or, of course – " began Jasleth.

Everybody else said "Ssh!" and several pages ran up and offered Maligna cream buns to put her in a better temper.

"Now," said Maligna, having changed the cream buns into large stones, "I'm going to give Jasleth and Goodness their presents."

There was a frightened hush.

"Just a little something each," said Maligna. "I should have done it at their christening, but I wasn't invited to that either. Was I?" she added to King Minus, who paled.

"Awfully kind of you," said Jasleth charmingly, "but really we couldn't accept –"

"Oh no," put in Goodness, over his shoulder, "really we couldn't."

"Too much already –" added Jasleth.

"Wouldn't dream of it –" added Goodness.

"Be quiet!" shouted Maligna. "That's better. Now then." She shook out her big black sleeves and clapped her hands. "Jasleth first. Come here, my dear."

Jasleth stepped half a pace forward, and Maligna yanked him the rest of the way.

"My present to Jasleth," said Maligna, "is that for one hour every day he will change into a raven –"

"Well!" exclaimed Jasleth, brightening up. "That's very kind of you –"

"However," added Maligna, giving him a friendly pat on the arm, "you'll never know when it's going to happen. Ha, ha."

"Ha, ha," echoed Jasleth weakly. The next moment he was gone, and there on the floor was a handsome black raven, looking rather surprised. "Oh, well," said the raven, and flew up on to the table to eat some birthday cake.

"And now for sweet little Goodness," said Maligna, smiling. Goodness burst into tears of fright. "I've decided," said Maligna, " to make her as good as she is beautiful, just right with her name." She pointed a long white finger at Goodness and shrieked, "From now on, Goodness will be so good that it will be silly!"

Everybody looked tremblingly at Goodness, but Goodness was smiling a happy smile. She turned and ran out, but in a few minutes she was back again, leading in all the sheep and goats, and some cows and oxen as well.

"Eat up, now," she encouraged them, and they buried their heads in the jelly. "Oh, Father," Goodness added, "we must ask all the kingdom's poor people up here and give them our clothes. They get so cold." She turned to the cook, and gave her three necklaces of rubies and emeralds, and her two crowns.

"Well, well," said Maligna sweetly. "I really must be away now," and she got into her serpent chariot, and whipped the serpents hard, just to remind them who it was. "By the way, I'm afraid these presents will only last for a year, until your next birthday in fact. Then let's see if you remember to ask me or not."

So saying, in a flash of lightning, wheels churning, and icing sugar showering in all directions, Maligna's chariot rushed out through the window, and back over the sea to her mountain.

"Goodness!" cried King Minus, but it was too late. His daughter was already running happily downstairs, out of the door, through the orchard, and into the town.

She stopped at all the houses.

"Follow me!" she cried. "I'm Princess Goodness, and I'm going to give you all sorts of lovely things to eat and wear."

All the beggars and poor people, and all the farmers and merchants and sailors too, came trooping after her, back to the palace.

"You can't possibly go on living in those nasty little houses," said Goodness. "Stay at the palace! Here's a pearl tiara for the baby. Just the right fit," she added

delightedly, helping one of the beggars into her
father's best purple, ermine-trimmed robe. "Oh,
Mother," she went on happily to the queen, "tomorrow I shall go out and ride through the kingdom,
and give everyone presents."

Prince Jasleth had taken a plate of cake in his beak,
and flown out through the window to join the owls
and storks who had been watching the proceed-
ings through the upper panes. They were most

sympathetic, though one of the younger storks did say, "I would have thought she might have turned you into something a bit more princely than *that*. Actually, a stork, I would have thought."

"Or an owl," said the owls.

"As a matter of fact," said one of the bats, "I thought she seemed quite a nice person. She did her hair rather well, you have to admit."

The sun sank down, bronze-red, and the stars shone out like little white flowers opening over the sea.

King Minus came tramping across the golden slates of the roof, calling out, "Jasleth! Jasleth! Where is the boy?"

"I'm here," said the raven, flying to King Minus' feet. "Sit down, Father, and have some cake."

King Minus sat among the storks and owls and bats.

"Just listen to it," he said.

Through the open window came the sound of beggars and poor people and farmers and merchants and sailors, and sheep, goats, cattle, pigs and oxen, all running about eating things, and trying things on, and knocking things over, and above all, Goodness' clear happy voice crying:

"Oh yes. That cloth of gold does look pretty, and wouldn't you like a nice sapphire brooch to set it off?"

"That it should come to this," sighed King Minus. "In a year, at this rate, my kingdom will be in ruins. Goodness is giving everything to the people. Soon your mother and I will be the only ones in rags."

"Ah, well," said Jasleth. "It can't be – "

Just then he changed back into a prince, and nearly fell off the roof. King Minus and one or two storks dragged him back.

26

"I'm afraid," said the king, "you'll have to go out and seek your fortune. You are our only hope, Jasleth."

Jasleth was still brushing himself down, and rubbing his arm where one of the storks had accidentally bitten him.

"Well, of course, Father, if you think it might help . . ." he said uncertainly. "If you really think . . ."

"Yes, yes," said the king. "It's the only answer. Besides, in the muddle we're going to be in for the next year or so, it won't be any help at all to have one's son changing into a raven every five minutes."

"No. I suppose not," said Jasleth, looking wistfully out at the well-known orchards, the slope with all the houses clinging on, and the darkening sea.

"There, there," said the king. "It will be the making of you."

"Can I take my horse?" asked Jasleth.

There was a steamy snort below them in the courtyard. Jasleth looked down from the roof and saw Goodness giving his horse to a delighted beggar.

"Oh, well," said Prince Jasleth with a sigh, "I'll just have to walk."

CHAPTER TWO

*In which Prince Jasleth sets out to seek his fortune,
and wishes he hadn't*

Prince Jasleth set out at first light. There were still a
few stars in the sky, and it was cold on the hills. He
had asked one of the beggars if he could borrow his old
patched cloak, as the beggar was now wearing a cloak
of red satin lined with fur. The beggar's cloak wasn't
very warm.

All the owls and storks and bats flew out to see him
off.

"Mind how you go," they cried.

A few of the bats even flew with him up into the
hills that marked the end of King Minus' kingdom.
They flapped around among the pines, where it was
always rather dark, and gave him lots of good advice
on the best places to hang upside down when he felt
sleepy. When the bats left him, and went flitting back
to the palace, Jasleth began to have real doubts about
the business.

After all, he thought, someone ought to be there to
look after Goodness. Here am I, out here, having a
good time – and he shivered – and poor Father and
Mother are back there in the warm, in dreadful
trouble. "I think I'll go back," he added to one of the
pine trees, "and get them to send the secretary in-

stead. He'd be much better at seeking his fortune than I am."

At this precise moment, he turned into a raven.

"I suppose that settles it," said the raven, gloomily.

He had half thought of tossing a coin – the beggar had given him a very small one, as he now had several gold pieces – to decide which direction to go in. However, ravens aren't very good at this, so he flew up above the pines, and went straight ahead.

'This isn't bad at all,' thought Jasleth, once he had got used to his wings, and stopped banging into pine tops. He could see all the woods and hills passing underneath, green and bluish in the distance, and rose-colour where the sun was just coming up and touching them. He saw a river, too, like a thread of silver, and followed it. Jasleth was so interested in everything that he forgot that his raven-ness only lasted an hour.

He was just flying happily over a big forest of oaks, when – whoosh! His wings vanished, his feathers vanished, the raven vanished, and, next moment, there was Prince Jasleth, in a rather ragged beggar's cloak, hurtling down towards the ground.

"I knew they should have sent the secretary," Jasleth remarked to all the leaves going past, and then "Ouch!" as the cloak caught on one of the branches a few feet from the ground, and Jasleth, instead of ending up with a lot of bruises and probably a few broken bones as well, was left hanging from an oak tree, upside down.

"Well!" exclaimed a large white owl, who lived in the tree, "I must say, you might have knocked."

"I beg your pardon," said Jasleth, still swinging up-side down.

"And it's customary," added the white owl, "to write beforehand and ask whether or not it's convenient to call."

"Well, I wasn't expecting to call, as a matter of fact," admitted Jasleth, making a grab at a branch, missing, grabbing again, and hauling himself up into the lower branches a second before his cloak gave way. "You don't happen to know where I am, do you?"

"You," said the white owl, "are in the Marvellous and Glorious Kingdom of King August, and you ought to be very thankful."

"Oh, I am," said Jasleth, thinking privately that the owl might have given him a wing-up.

"Just round those big oaks over there," said the owl, "you'll see a splendid building with a blue roof and silver pillars. *That's* King August's palace."

"Fine," said Jasleth. "Thank you."

He climbed down the tree to the mossy ground between the oak roots. There was a little pool near by, and Jasleth caught sight of himself in it. He looked a mess. Apart from the fact that Goodness had given all his really nice things away, and he had come out in his eighth-best, he now had leaves and bits of twig stuck all over him and in his black hair, and there were green stains on his face and clothes. His boots were all muddy from the rather wet ground (they must have had some rain earlier, or perhaps it was only heavy dew), and as for his cloak – well! He wondered if he ought to take it off, but as it hid some of the stains and other tears, he decided not to. He washed his face, and clawed at his hair, which made things worse, then turned resolutely towards the palace which he could see by now through the trees. It was a very nice palace, with lots of figures carved out of stone standing on the steps, and there were no sheep, and not one goat.

Jasleth went boldly up to the big door and knocked the massive silver knocker which was shaped like a panther's head.

The door shot open at once and out stepped a small, tubby herald with a trumpet, all ready to blow.

"If you've come for the rubbish," said the herald pompously, "it's round the back."

"I haven't," said Jasleth. "I've come to see the king."

The herald screamed with laughter.

"Look here – " said Jasleth.

"I am," said the herald, "and I must say, you *do* look a sight."

Jasleth decided it was better not to punch the herald in the eye before he got to see the king. It might not make a good impression.

"*I*," said Jasleth, "am Prince Jasleth, son of King Minus."

"King of what?" chortled the herald. "The pig trough?"

Jasleth promptly elbowed the herald out of the way, and strode into the big hall inside. The herald ran in after him, shouting, but he was so tubby he soon got out of breath. There was no one in the first hall, apart from a couple of small dolphin playing about in a large pool, who went out of their way to splash him from head to foot as he went past. However, they splashed the herald, too.

In the next hall, King August was sitting at his silver table, eating his breakfast with all his lords and ladies, and his daughter. They were all passing each other toast, and cracking boiled eggs.

The herald threw himself on his face, begging everybody's pardon for letting Jasleth in.

"I am Prince Jasleth," said the prince, as soon as he could get a word in edgeways.

Everybody round the table burst into peals of laughter. The princess, King August's daughter, laughed harder than anyone else.

"I will forgive your presumption," gasped King

August, "because there's nothing I like better than a good laugh." He wiped his eyes. "Now. I suppose you've come about cleaning the cellars."

"I've come," said Prince Jasleth, "to seek my fortune."

This started them all off again.

"It so happens that I fell into an oak tree," explained the prince, and wished he hadn't. He decided to wait until they had finished rolling all over the table.

Eventually, King August wiped his eyes again, this time with his toast, and said:

"Now. I'll get somebody to show you where the cellars are."

"Look here," said Jasleth, "haven't you got an awful monster I could slay for you, or something? One with six legs and a serpent's tail, and a lion's head, breathing out fire – "

"Oh," said King August, "you're too late for that. We had that thing got rid of last week."

"Well, how about your daughter? I could rescue her from something –"

Jasleth broke off to duck as the princess threw the toast rack at him. It hit the herald.

"Fancy throwing a toast rack," said Jasleth. "There are lots of other things – how about your egg, for example?"

He ducked again.

"Or the jam pot?"

The herald got this too, and it was open. He was all sticky and eggy and breathless.

"Hmm," said Jasleth. "What a sight you look."

And he walked out of the palace and down the steps.

"I knew," thought Jasleth, "that the secretary should have come instead." He went back among the oak trees.

It was a very upsetting sort of day.

For one thing, nobody believed him when he told them he was a prince, which was a bit annoying when up till now everybody had always *known* without being told. For another, there seemed to be no way at all of seeking a fortune. There was a shortage of monsters for a start, although once, about lunchtime, Jasleth came out of the oak wood into a big meadow, and there was a royally dressed young man, obviously a prince because he was wearing a golden crown, running after a scaly thing with two heads.

"Ah!" cried Jasleth, his heart lifting. "A battle at last. Can I help at all?" he yelled to the prince.

Both the prince and the scaly thing turned and stared at him in surprise.

"Help with what?" asked the prince.

"Help you slay that monster," offered Jasleth.

Both the monster's two heads turned bright pink, and all its four big eyes screwed up, and it burst into tears. The prince with the crown picked it up in his arms at once, and said indignantly to Jasleth:

"How dare you frighten my pet! (There! There!) Anyone could see we were only playing."

A bit later he came to a little white house in the middle of some orchards, and knocked at the door to ask if they could spare him some food. He was rather hungry. He hadn't even had any breakfast – all the beggars had eaten it.

The people in the white house gave him some cheese

34

and three apples, which he soon ate, but when he asked them if he could rescue anyone for them, or if they knew where there might be some hidden treasure, or a large, fierce monster with seven heads and six tails, they said everything like that had been done years ago, but he could help them pick the apples if he liked. Prince Jasleth had often heard that tasks like this led into wonderful adventures. He might find a magic ring in an apple, or a princess changed into a tree. However, everything was depressingly normal, and the people who owned the orchards soon got tired of his cutting open all the apples to look for magic rings, and going up to the trees and saying, "How do you do; can I be of any help?"

Towards evening, Jasleth came out of a wood, and found that he was standing on a hill-top, looking down at the dark blue sea. There was a little town under the hill, and some boats moored at the water's edge, and, further out, a big timber ship, with a mermaid painted on her side, and a scarlet sail.

Well, thought Jasleth sensibly, if there's no fortune-seeking to be had over here, there might be plenty over *there*, and he looked out across the sea to the place where he thought the opposite shore might be.

He went down into the town, and found the sailors from the ship, and asked them if they would take him over.

"Well," said one of the sailors, "we don't usually take passengers, you understand, but if you're willing to pull an oar –"

"Pull an oar where?" inquired Jasleth.

The sailor said something which Jasleth considered

rather rude. He then took Jasleth aboard the mermaid ship, and showed him what he meant. He meant sitting on a hard wooden bench, and taking a long rough oar in his hands, and dragging it up and forwards a certain number of times every minute to keep the ship moving.

"It's very kind of you," said Jasleth. "Thank you. I'll do it. There is just one thing. . . ."

"Oh yes?"

"You see," said Jasleth, trying to appear as if he didn't mind, and as if it were quite usual for things like this to happen in the place he came from, "I change into a raven for an hour every day."

"Bless me."

"Bless you," said the prince, obligingly.

Next day, just after dawn, having shivered all night long on the *Mermaid*'s deck, Jasleth joined everybody else at the oars. It was very hard work and very painful, and it was almost a relief when he changed into a raven, and could go and sit up on the mast. The sailors, however, weren't terribly pleased at having to man his oar as well as their own. When the hour was up, they all scowled at him as he fell down from the mast.

"Never thought you *meant* it," said the first sailor reproachfully.

As soon as it got dark, they put down anchor. Jasleth was so stiff and sore that he groaned aloud every time he turned over in his sleep, and everybody told him to be quiet. He dreamed, between his groans, of being at home with King Minus and the queen and Princess Goodness and the secretary and his horse. In his dream, Goodness thought he was a beggar, and was kindly giving him his crown and all his own things by mistake.

He was woken up by a rough shake, and a piece of bread and cheese, and very soon they were off again.

They passed a few mermaids on a little island of rock, all covered with green seaweed, and with creamy shells in their long blue hair. The mermaids laughed and pointed rudely. Jasleth was a bit disappointed that they weren't more romantic. He had always thought they sat around combing their hair and singing sweet songs. They were actually combing their hair, but they kept screaming "Ooch!" and "Ooh!" whenever they got a tangle.

At this point in Jasleth's adventures, Maligna, the dreadful enchantress, was picking up her magic looking-glass. It was a wonderful thing that could talk, and looked just like an ordinary mirror until you said the right spell. Then it showed you any place in the world that you wanted to look at.

"*Mirror, mirror, in my hand,*" chanted Maligna, "*Who is the fairest in the land?*"

"You are," said the mirror politely.

"And who are the sweetest little bats?"

"The bats in your hair are," said the mirror.

"And who are the dearest, darlingest two wolfies anybody could hope to have?"

"Sweetie and Poppet," said the mirror, in a weary voice.

Sweetie and Poppet rubbed their rough, black sides against Maligna and wagged their tails. The mirror thought it was all quite sickening.

"Now," said Maligna briskly, "let's see how Minus is getting on," and she said the spell.

Minus' palace appeared in the mirror. It was full of animals and people. Goodness was bustling about, and carrying roast chicken and peaches and cream to the poor people, as they sat on ivory chairs. She wore an old darned dress that the cook had given her in exchange for her cloth-of-gold. The dress was really too big, and every so often Goodness tripped on its hem and fell over on top of a sheep or a beggar. King Minus and the queen and the secretary were all sitting in the corner, eating some stale bread, and looking rather miserable.

Maligna was just giving Sweetie and Poppet a particularly affectionate kick out of pure joy, when she noticed that Jasleth wasn't there.

She made the mirror show her every inch of the palace, and then of the kingdom. Then at last, when it was getting dark, and the moon was rising over the woods, she spotted in her mirror a ship with a mermaid painted on the side, lying at anchor in a calm sea. What caught her attention was a young man who was falling on to the deck from quite high up, in a shower of raven feathers.

"Ah!" screamed Maligna. "So! Ah! Ah! Ho!"

Sweetie and Poppet looked at each other nervously, and wondered if they ought to go out and bite another postman somewhere to cheer her up. Maligna, however, was not so upset as she seemed.

"Now I've got you," she cried at last. "I'll make you wish you'd never left home, dear Jasleth."

So saying, she flapped her way up to the top of her

crooked palace, and began to stir her smelliest cauldron, and poke about in her nastiest spell books.

"What have we here? A dragon's milk tooth! In it
goes!"

She laughed happily, and there was a lot of
bubbling and hissing from the cauldron. Her omelettes
were just as bad.

It wasn't till morning that the horrible storm that
Maligna had conjured up came bounding across the
sea to the mermaid ship.

The clouds were big and dull green, and the wind roared. Fairly soon huge waves lashed up and threw the ship first one way and then another. A couple of sea-serpents hurried by, holding umbrellas to keep off the pelting rain.

The storm had woken Jasleth up before anyone else, but he couldn't bale out the water in buckets when they asked him to.

"I'm afraid I'm rather busy, just at the moment," he said.

He was busy being sick over the side.

Everybody grumbled and the ship tossed, and Jasleth groaned. Somebody had once told him that if you lay flat on your back when you felt sick, it made you feel rather better. When he tried this, the ship gave a great heave, and he rolled all the way down the deck into the rowers, and everybody fell over backwards.

"This is no time to play games," grumbled all the sailors.

When the sail split wide open a few minutes later, they decided that Jasleth had brought them bad luck, and the best thing to do was to throw him overboard into the sea.

"Oh, come now," said Jasleth, as they picked him up, just as if they were going to give him bumps, "you can't – "

"One!" roared the sailors, swinging him.

"I say, just look at that funny-shaped cloud," cried Jasleth, trying to distract their attention. "Just like a – "

"Two!" sang the sailors.

"Just like a-a-hippopotamus – or a – "

"Three!"

"Gir-aaaffe!" yelled Jasleth, as he found himself flying through the air towards the waves.

Just then, luckily, he had his daily enchanted hour and changed into a raven.

Ignoring the sailors, who were shouting and yelling at him, he turned and flew through the storm, over the leaping water, battered all the time by the wind. He seemed to fly for a long while, and he was hoping that his hour wasn't up yet. It would be no joke to change back into a prince and fall into that angry sea. Just as he was thinking this, he saw a line of land lying in front of him. He flew on towards it as fast as his wings would carry him, and gradually, as he got nearer, he could see the forest slopes and hills rising from the shore.

No sooner had he come gasping and flapping in over the beach than he changed back into Jasleth the prince, and fell into the wet sand, head first.

It was still raining rather hard, but it helped to wash the sand out of his eyes and ears and mouth.

"I don't know where I am," he thought, "but it must be somewhere or I suppose I wouldn't be here."

He looked around for someone to ask, but the only thing he saw was a big crab sitting in a rock pool, who put in ear-plugs, and refused to answer.

So Jasleth began to walk up the beach into the forest at the top. He walked and walked. Gradually the rain stopped beating on the branches overhead, and the sun came out and shone through in long golden shafts. Jasleth began to feel a bit happier about things. He also began to feel hungry. Pretty soon he came to a cottage with a thatched roof, and out of the cottage came curling the most wonderful breakfast smells Jasleth thought he had ever smelled. He went up the path and knocked on the door.

A tiny woman in an apron looked out. He didn't have to say a word.

"Oh, you poor, dear boy," cried the tiny woman. "Come in, come in."

Jasleth did as she said, and fairly soon he was sitting at her table eating his way through an enormous plate of eggs and bacon and tomatoes.

"Now," said the tiny woman, as he went on to new bread and honey, "you must tell me who you are, and where you are going."

"I am a – " Jasleth had been going to say he was a prince but thought better of it. "I'm a farmer's son," he said instead, "setting out to seek my fortune."

The tiny woman laughed.

"I thought so," she said. "There were three through here yesterday. I suppose you're thinking of joining King Purple's son."

"No – er – well," said Jasleth. "Joining him at what?"

"Oh!" cried the tiny woman. "Haven't you heard? I was sure you must have come because of that."

"Of what?"

"King Purple's son, Prince Fearless, is setting off on a quest in a great ship. He's called on all the able-bodied young men to help him."

Prince Jasleth was so delighted about this he hardly knew where to begin with all the questions he wanted to ask. Eventually he said:

"A quest for what?"

"Ah," said the tiny woman, "For the *Dragon Hoard*."

"Which?" asked Jasleth.

"I suppose, being a stranger, you might not have heard," said the tiny woman, rather as if she thought he *must* have heard, and was just being silly about it. Then she told him.

The Dragon Hoard was a fantastic treasure that had belonged to King Purple's kingdom in the first place. An important dragon had presented it to King Purple's great-great-great-great-grandfather, and then agreed to guard it for him. But it was a forgetful sort of dragon, and one day it thought of someone it wanted to see, and flew off, and didn't remember to come back. A bad-tempered old enchanter called Stamp-Weed had promptly carried off the Hoard and given it to the king of a far-off land in order to get the king's friendship and help for some nasty reason or another. From then on, the treasure had been passed from king to king. By now, nobody in King Purple's kingdom knew what it was, or even what it looked like. They did know, however, which kingdom Stamp-Weed had taken it to. Prince Fearless apparently thought it was about time somebody got it back for King Purple, who was its rightful owner, after all.

"And this far-off kingdom," asked Jasleth. "How far off is it?"

"Oh," said the tiny woman, "some people say it's at the end of the earth. At best, it would probably take half a year to get there, and half a year to get back."

Jasleth ate up the last of the bread and honey. This

sounded like a real adventure at last, and a real chance of finding his fortune and saving his father, King Minus, from ruin. Then he remembered his rather messy clothes and the leaves still stuck in his hair.

The tiny woman seemed to guess what he was thinking.

"I have to go out and feed the squirrels soon," she said. "I'll heat some water, and while I'm gone you can have a bath. We'll brush your clothes down and comb your hair, and you'll look as good as new."

Jasleth was very grateful.

He had a bath in a wooden tub, and when he put on his clothes, he found them all neatly darned, and brushed clean of all the mud and moss stains.

The tiny woman also gave him a scarlet cloak, which she took out of a cupboard. She threw the beggar's cloak away. When he had washed his hair and combed all the sea-salt and twigs out of it he looked marvellous; almost like a prince again, and certainly very noble and handsome.

"Here is the address of my brother," said the tiny woman, as he set off. "It will take you two days to reach King Purple's palace, following the road, and my brother will see you have a bed for the night in between, and here are some sausage sandwiches."

Jasleth was so grateful he hardly knew what to say to the tiny woman for all her kindness.

He kissed her on the cheek instead of saying anything.

"There, there," said the tiny woman. "Enjoy your adventure."

And she waved him out of sight.

CHAPTER THREE

*In which Prince Fearless receives an
enchanted sign*

It was a pleasant journey. For a lot of the way the
road ran through the woods. The leaves were so thick
overhead that the sunlight came through them
coloured green, and it was like walking under the sea.
At other times Jasleth went past cornfields, over
bridges, and through a small village or two. When he
changed into a raven at noon he was able to give his
feet a rest.

The sun was just making up its mind to fall down
behind some hills, when Jasleth arrived at the house
of the tiny woman's brother. It was exactly as she had
described it, with a red roof and shutters, and ten
poplars growing all round it.

Jasleth knocked at the door.

A big stout man opened it, and looked at Jasleth
without much pleasure.

"I met your sister in the wood," Jasleth said,
"and she told me you might very kindly be able
to – "

"She did, did she?" The stout man scowled. "She's
always doing it. It's too bad of her. People I've never
met charging in here at all hours. Oh, well, I suppose
I should be thankful there's only one of you. Yesterday
there were three."

He led Jasleth inside, and gave him some soup, and a bed in the attic. Once he was in bed, Jasleth could hear all the spiders up in the beams and the mice in the walls whispering about him.

"Who is it tonight?"

"Can't see; he's blown the candle out. Thought he had black hair."

They went on talking all night long, and Jasleth didn't get a wink of sleep.

In the morning he chopped some wood for the tiny woman's brother, to say "thank you", and went on his way without waiting for breakfast.

Within a short time he realised this was a mistake, but he walked bravely along, whistling. He still had his splendid scarlet cloak, after all, and he still looked handsome enough to go out on a quest.

Unfortunately, Aunt (or Cousin) Maligna was looking in her magic mirror again. She had found out how Jasleth had escaped the storm, and she was furious. Sweetie and Poppet had run out and hidden in the woods in fright as she hurled things about and screamed at the top of her voice, which she always did when she was feeling particularly angry. She even gave the bats a good comb.

When eventually she found where Jasleth had got to, and saw him walking happily along towards the palace of King Purple, in his scarlet cloak, whistling, she nearly smashed the looking-glass. However, just before she did, she realised what he was up to. She had heard about the quest for the Dragon Hoard, and of course she knew all about the Hoard itself. Enchanters live for a very long time, and she had known the nasty Stamp-Weed; dear old Stampy-Puss she always called him.

"I'll soon put a stop to *this*!" she declared in ringing tones, and, encouraged, Sweetie and Poppet came loping back to the palace. "Stop snivelling!" she added to the bats. "Or I'll perm the lot of you!"

There was silence.

"Now," said Maligna, stirring her cauldron, with a revolting smile.

Jasleth had just seen the town and the palace in the middle of it, on a little rise, down in the valley below him. Beyond the town lay the long white beach and the glittering blue sea. It reminded him so much of home, that his heart was even higher than before, when it suddenly started to teem with rain.

There wasn't a bit of cover for miles; he'd left the woods a long way back. Besides, this rain was a particularly unpleasant, muddy sort of rain. It made black stains on his beautiful cloak, and he was already soaked through. He went and stood under the only tree he could see on the hillside, but it wasn't much of a tree, and the muddy rain poured through the branches.

When at last the torrent stopped, Jasleth saw that his boots were caked with mud, his clothes were filthy again, and his face was probably as dirty as everything else. To add to all the other troubles, his cloak had a great hole in it where one of the branches of the tree had torn it.

Nobody was going to take him on the quest for the Dragon Hoard when he looked like this.

Jasleth could have cried.

47

He didn't have a chance to, however. The next moment he had changed into a raven.

"This is the last straw," said the raven.

And then he had an idea.

It was one of those wonderful ideas that sometimes come when there really doesn't seem to be any way out of your troubles. It lit up Jasleth's gloom like a flash of lightning. Of course, he had heard often enough of enchanted signs being given to people to show them what they should do, like the time his own great-grandfather had come to a crossroads and not known which road to choose, when all of a sudden his horse had broken into a gallop and gone down the road on the left, thereby choosing for him. Jasleth thought his idea was splendid. He flew up from the muddy ground and flapped down the hill to the valley, and across the valley to the little town round the palace of King Purple, and into the market place.

The market place, one end of which sloped down into the harbour, was full of people all running about and laughing and shouting and complaining. There were lots of stalls under coloured awnings, but nobody seemed to be taking much notice of these. Up at the far end, looking out towards the water, was a painted wooden dais, with a purple canopy. At the dais was a flustered-looking person with a pen and a long list, who was obviously a secretary, and next to him, looking rather grand and pleased, was a handsome, blond young man in royal robes – clearly Prince Fearless. As Jasleth flew in, a long line of youths was filing past the flustered secretary, giving their names and their reasons for wanting to go on the quest. The secretary was scribbling wildly.

"Please don't gabble!" he kept saying, almost tear-fully. "And please don't go so *fast*. *Who* did you say you were?"

Prince Jasleth didn't wait for the right opportunity. He simply flew in between the queue and landed on the secretary's inkwell, which he knocked over. The ink went everywhere, especially over the secretary's boots.

Prince Fearless jumped up angrily.

"Guard!" he cried. "Arrest this raven at once! This is not," he added to Jasleth, "the place to come for breadcrumbs."

"I do beg your pardon, your highness," said the raven, "but I'm an enchanted raven. I've brought you a sign about your quest."

Prince Fearless looked excited. He was a very romantic sort of prince, and thought an enchanted sign would be just the thing to send the quest off properly.

"All right, guard," he said. "You can go away again. Well?"

"I have to tell you, Prince Fearless, that your quest will only be a success if you have with you a certain king's son named Jasleth. He will bring you good luck, and without him you won't get the Dragon Hoard."

Prince Fearless paled. He dug the secretary in the ribs, and cried:

"Check the list!"

The secretary checked. He shook his head.

"Nobody here called Jasleth, Prince Fearless."

"There must be! Let me look!"

Fearless checked too, and turned paler. All the people chattered and asked what the matter was.

49

"What shall I do?" implored Fearless. "My beautiful quest – ruined!"

"Perhaps," said the raven, "Jasleth hasn't arrived yet."

"Ah!" cried Fearless, looking better. "But how shall I know him when I see him?"

"Oh, you can't miss him," said the raven. "He's covered in mud, and he has a big tear in his cloak. It's a task he had to do," the raven added hastily as Prince Fearless looked pale again. "You see, a wicked enchantress put a spell on his sister, and, to break it, the prince had to travel seven days dressed as a beggar, and covered in mud. Today the seven days are up. Of course," concluded the raven, "he may not pass your town at all."

Fearless started to gnaw his fingernails.

The raven flew up from the dais and over the market place and out of the town. He had just cleared the gate when – whoosh! He changed back into Prince Jasleth, and fell into another tree.

"I should have said two tears in the cloak," Jasleth muttered to himself, climbing down. "And the toe of one boot missing," he added sourly.

He went in through the gate again, and as soon as he started down the main street, a crowd came rushing out and surrounded him.

"Prince Jasleth!" they cried. "At last!"

"Why, how clever of you to know my name," said Jasleth, pretending to be all innocent and surprised. "Or was it just a good guess?"

"Come along! Come along!" and Jasleth was bustled towards the market place.

Poor Prince Fearless was by now in an awful state.

51

He was pacing up and down the dais, muttering, and the secretary was sobbing into a bright yellow hanky.

"Here he is!" screamed the crowd.

Prince Fearless came bounding down the steps, and embraced Jasleth like a long-lost friend.

"My dear fellow!" cried Fearless, and then drew back, trying not to look dismayed at being covered with dry mud.

"Er . . ." said Prince Jasleth.

"We've been waiting for you," said Prince Fearless. "Congratulations. I hope your sister's much better."

"Why, however did you know about that . . ."

"Ah!" Fearless waved a playful finger. "Come along. I'll find you some more suitable clothes at the palace."

King Purple's palace was made of marble overlaid with gold, and the roof was decorated with amethysts. The bath was a huge hollowed-out diamond. Jasleth was rather impressed.

"Of course," said Prince Fearless, "you'll join our quest, won't you?"

"Well, after you've been so kind, how could I possibly refuse?" asked Jasleth, admiring his new cloth-of-gold cloak, embroidered with peacocks.

"You're the last one," said Fearless, as they went down the gold staircase to dinner. "The fiftieth rower. You can row, can't you?"

"Oh, yes," said Jasleth proudly.

"Our ship isn't quite ready yet, but she's a real beauty. I'll take you down to see her in the morning."

In King Purple's hall the other forty-eight rowers, all looking splendid, were sitting at the long golden table, tucking into turkey and stuffing. King Purple himself sat on his throne, looking rather bored with everything except the turkey.

"This is Prince Jasleth, Father," said Prince Fearless.

"How do you do, my boy," said King Purple. "You're going on this quest thing too, are you? Silly idea."

Prince Jasleth was shocked.

"I thought, your majesty, that the Dragon Hoard was your rightful property," he said.

"Mmm? Oh, yes. Suppose it is. Have some baked potatoes."

Jasleth was also introduced to Prince Fearless' sister, Princess Poppy-Lily. She was a disappointing princess. She had golden hair, but was rather plump, which she wasn't helping by gobbling up all the food she could lay her hands on. If she saw something she particularly wanted when she was in the middle of eating something else, she made one of the servants go and mark it with a special little flag on a pin which said: *Reserved for the Princess*. She had three tame peacocks who sat round and gossiped with her, and pecked from her fingers very noisily. They immediately started to fight with the embroidered peacocks on Jasleth's cloak. Prince Fearless and two heralds rescued him. Princess Poppy-Lily giggled.

During dinner one of the heralds marched into the middle of the hall, and announced:

"Hear ye all! Hear ye all! Noble company of princes, lords and gentlemen!"

"Why can't the fellow get on with it?" said King Purple in a loud voice.

"By the wish of Prince Fearless," cried the herald, rather red about the ears, "all who go with him on the quest will be given a share of the treasure, and the noblest may win the hand of the beautiful Princess Poppy-Lily."

"But you don't have to, if you'd rather not," hissed Prince Fearless in Jasleth's ear. "That's only Father's idea. Pass it on."

Unfortunately the message got a bit jumbled up going down the long table, so that the last rower, a king's son from somewhere, named Sillius, stood up and asked what —

"Buttered on one toe if you drove a nut. That's sunny for the side ear. Parsley scone"

— meant.

Next morning Prince Fearless took Jasleth down to the boatyard to look at his ship. It was called, of course, *The Quest*, and was gilded all over, with a huge goldfish painted on each side at the front. Even the mast was plated over with gold, and the sail was going to be bright orange with a picture of a cask with handles on it. This was supposed to be the receptacle that the Dragon Hoard was in, although no one knew for sure.

"We haven't got a figurehead yet," said Fearless. "I think we ought to have a mermaid or something like that."

"No," said Jasleth, remembering those he had seen. "Definitely not a mermaid."

"Careful with that oar!" yelled Fearless. "Excuse me." He went on deck to tell someone off, and just as well too. At that moment Jasleth changed into his

daily raven. Naturally he didn't want Fearless, or any of the others, to know that this happened, as it would give the game away about the "enchanted sign". Feeling rather ashamed of himself, Jasleth flew off to the beach to sit and watch the sea rolling in and out until he became a prince again.

"Jasleth!" he could hear Fearless calling worriedly. "Where are you, Jasleth?"

Alas, Maligna had been watching his adventures since she had thrown that muddy rain over him. Now she was in a dreadful fury. Sweetie and Poppet were biting people all over the mountain to try to put her in a better mood, and her black toad, who looked out through the peep-hole by the door, had hopped all the way upstairs to tell her a cheering story about his shortsighted old aunt, who had mistaken him for a toadstool. Maligna had ungratefully picked him up, and thrown him out of the window into the pond.

When she quietened down a bit, however, she began to think up a splendid plan. She dressed herself up as a little old woman with white hair and a stick and a long cloak, and practised a simper or two in what she thought was a kindly fashion. She was rather good at dressing up, and, if you hadn't known it was Maligna, you really might have thought that here was a sweet little old lady, who perhaps would give you a sweet or an apple, instead of hitting you on the nose with her stick, or changing you into a hippopotamus. Then she said a few spells, threw some magic dust over herself, and disappeared from the room.

She reappeared on the beach not far from the place where Jasleth was standing, digging in the sand with his beak to help out a starfish that had got stuck.

"Aah, good morning, dear little blackbird," quavered Maligna. "What a pity I haven't any crumbs left. I gave them all to the gulls up the beach."

"Thank you, that's quite all right," said Jasleth. "And, as a matter of fact, I'm a raven not a black-bird."

"Dear, dear," said Maligna, still quavering, "my eyesight gets worse every day. I know a thing or two, though. Oh yes, indeed. Take young Prince Fearless now; what a fine young man! And he wants a figure-head for his ship, doesn't he? Well, you see that log down the beach, washed up by the tide. Well, if he were to make a figurehead out of *that* now. My, my!"

"What would happen?" asked Jasleth, not surprisingly rather interested.

"You see," said the little old woman, "I happen to know that log's part of a magic tree. Could tell it at a glance. If the prince took it, and carved it into a human shape, it would speak, and give him lots of good advice. Ah, well," sighed Maligna, hobbling on up the beach. "Must be getting back to my sweet little cottage, and my dear little dicky-birds."

As soon as she was round the rocks, she looked into a rock pool, and pulled a face at a couple of crabs that gave them bad dreams for a week.

Jasleth was hopping about with excitement. As soon as he had changed into a prince again, he ran back to the boatyard, where the carpenters and heralds and Prince Fearless were scrambling all over the place, looking into barrels and under benches for him. Fearless was just giving the order to take up all the planks in the ship's bottom, when he caught sight of Jasleth.

"Wherever have you been?" he cried.

Jasleth told him that a raven had beckoned him with its wing, and showed him a magic log lying on the beach, which, if carved into human shape, would speak and give lots of good advice.

Naturally, Prince Fearless had the log hauled up to the boatyard, and soon the chief carpenter had carved it into the form of a beautiful young woman with long hair. It was painted and gilded and, to be truthful, a nicer figurehead would have been hard to come by.

Except, of course, that it was not in the least bit magic. Maligna intended to speak through the figure-head herself, and give the worst advice she could think of.

She did not intend the quest to be successful.

PART TWO

The Quest

CHAPTER FOUR

*In which the magic log sends the ship in the wrong
direction, and Jasleth eats a stone bun*

Everyone came to see them off.

The populace stood on the quay and threw roses
and waved flags and shouted "Hurrah!" The royal
trumpeters trumpeted, and the royal drummers
drummed, and between them nearly sent everybody
deaf. *The Quest* waited on the water, looking marvellous with its bright orange sails. Even King Purple
came grumbling down to the harbour, wrapped up in
a purple cloak with his crown on rather crookedly.

"Now," he said, snappishly, to his son, "what is it
that I have had to be dragged out of a warm bed to
do, eh?"

Prince Fearless, looking rather embarrassed,
muttered:

"You're supposed to give us your blessing and wish
us luck."

King Purple raised his voice to a loud boom, and
roared:

"Bless you all, all fifty – or is it forty-nine? – of you!
And the best of luck! I won't wave you off," he added
to Prince Fearless. "Don't want cook to burn the toast
again," and so saying, he went back to the palace and
shut the door.

61

Prince Fearless cleared his throat, and made a grand speech to the populace about how brave and noble all the fifty rowers were, which included him, too, of course, and how they would soon come back bearing the Dragon Hoard with them. Everyone cheered and threw roses. Someone threw a flag by mistake and made Prince Sillius' nose bleed. Otherwise everything went off all right until *The Quest* had been boarded.

The fifty youths strained gallantly at their oars, and the ship swung out of the harbour towards the open sea.

Just as the sail caught the breeze, and Prince Fearless was leaving his oar in order to say a few final important and romantic words to the people from the stern, Princess Poppy-Lily, who was still slinging roses into the water, overbalanced and fell in with a huge splash. Her three peacocks went into hysterics and five strong heralds dived into the harbour to fish her out. She really was a rather heavy princess, especially with her crown and all her jewels on, not to mention her flounced skirt and fan and rose-basket that she obstinately clung to all the time she was in the water.

What with all the flurry and disturbance and noise, the going of *The Quest* was completely ignored.

The last thing Jasleth saw was King Purple up on the roof of the palace feeding some eagles, and obviously telling them that this business of the Dragon Hoard was utter nonsense.

Maligna naturally was watching all this in her looking-glass. She didn't intend to let the ship out of her nasty sight for a second. When she went away to make a cup of stinging-nettle tea, or something like

that, she made her black toad come up and watch instead, and tell her what had happened. The toad, who caught a bad cold from being thrown in the pond, had its feet in a mustard bath most of the time, and was wrapped up in a big black eiderdown. It had lots of black handkerchiefs into which it sneezed and coughed and sniffled, and lots of bottles of cough-mixture and nose-drops, and things to rub on its chest, and things to swallow three times a day, and things that should only be taken at night. Wherever it went, it carted all its bottles and eiderdowns and hankies and mustard baths with it, which made an awful clanking and rattling noise. Maligna kept thinking it was one of her old ghost friends dragging chains around with it, and rushing out to say "Hallo". It was always the toad, of course, and then Maligna would stick him head first in the mustard and pour his nose-drops and cough mixture all over his eiderdown, and tell him not to pretend to be people he wasn't.

At the moment, Maligna was in fact rather pleased. She had seen that, although *The Quest* was sailing on a calm blue sea, there was a dreadful storm blowing up that would hit the ship about sunset. When Prince Fearless inquired from the magic log if they were going the right way, Maligna, using her sweetest voice, assured him that they were, and that, despite a tiny bit of possible bother about evening, all would be well.

Prince Jasleth, meanwhile, was having a worrying time trying not to let the other questors see him change into a raven. Every time he thought it felt as though he might be, he leaped up from his oar, and raced down into the ship's hold where all the food was stored, and it was nice and dark.

"Where are you off to, Jasleth?" inquired Prince Onga. Onga was a huge black prince from a far-away land, who insisted on wearing his feathered headdress all the time. The rowers who sat behind him complained that they couldn't see where they were going.

"Er – off to?" stuttered Jasleth. "I thought I heard something b-barging ab-bout in the hold – was going to, er, have a look, er –"

64

"In the hold?" purred Onga in his black velvet voice. "I'll come with you, Jasleth. Might be a leopard!" There was an unmistakable twinkle in his eye. "Or a panther!"

"I think," said Jasleth, "it's a raven," and fled.

Of course, he didn't change into a raven then, and as the day went by he got more and more nervous. He was certain that Fearless would realise at once that a prince who turned into a raven must have played that trick of the "enchanted sign" on him. He would probably throw Jasleth overboard.

Just before sunset a strong wind blew up and punched at the sail. The seas turned green and choppy, and black clouds swallowed up the sinking sun.

"This must be the spot of bother the magic log warned us about," said Fearless, and the next moment a great wave rushed over the side and soaked him.

It was a dreadful storm. The waves were like towers with feet that kicked *The Quest* back and forth as though trying to score a goal with it. They had to take down the sail before it was torn in half, and pull in the oars before they were dragged out of the rowers' hands. They tied everything down to the deck and hoped for the best. Prince Jasleth was even too scared to be sick, although Prince Sillius wasn't. They had to bale, too, throwing out the water in buckets, but the sea kept pouring more in.

In the middle of all this, Jasleth changed into a raven. Luckily everyone was too busy to notice. He felt rather guilty about not helping, but there was nothing he could do in his present shape. He thought it might be a good idea to see if there was any land around, as the storm was blowing them wildly off course, so he circled round and round under the clouds, and looked in all directions, but there was no land to be seen.

An albatross flew by.

"Terrible weather we're having lately," it remarked to Jasleth.

"You don't happen to know of any islands around here," said Jasleth. "Or even where 'here' is?"

"Goodness me!" said the albatross. "'Here' is here, of course. Down there's the sea, and up here's the sky. That's all I know, and all I want to know, too, I'm sure."

"Thank you," said Jasleth.

"Don't mention it," said the albatross.

By the time Jasleth fell back into the ship an hour later, the storm had quietened down, although it was still raining, and the thunder was booming away to itself in the distance.

Some of the rowers said it was Onga's fault that they were lost, and if he had taken his feathers off, they would have been able to see where they were going. Onga laughed.

"The best thing to do," said Fearless, "is to ask the magic log."

He went down the deck to the prow and up to where the carved woman was leaning out towards the sea.

"Excuse me, oh magic log," began Fearless.

"Yes, my dear," said the log, in its most syrupy voice.

"We wondered if you could tell us which way to

go. We were blown off course, you see, in that little bit of bother back there."

The log gave a tinkling laugh.

"Rather fun, wasn't it?" it cried.

"Oh, yes," agreed Fearless gallantly, not wanting to hurt the log's feelings.

"Well, now – " said the log, and told him the best way for them to go. It was quite the wrong way, going in practically the opposite direction to the land with the Dragon Hoard, but naturally Fearless couldn't know this. He thanked it, and went and told the rowers. Everybody cheered, and they sailed happily even further off course.

Dawn turned the sea to pale gold, and a school of dolphin went by with their maths master, all crying:

"Five by five is twenty – er – " and blowing water spouts.

On the horizon there could now be seen the little dark hump of an island.

"I think we'll put in there," said Fearless, "and get some fresh water, and see if they know anything about the Dragon Hoard."

When they sailed into the bay, they began to see that it was a funny sort of island. It was all grey and rather shiny, like polished stone. When they left the ship to walk over the sand dunes, they found that it *was* polished stone. The sand was stone, and the grass was stone, and at the top of the beach, all the trees and flowers and bushes were stone too. There was a stone waterfall and a stone stream, and, as they went on, worse and worse, little stone monkeys and squirrels and birds, holding stone nuts and stone oranges in their stone beaks and paws.

They came to a big clearing in the woods, and saw a big stone palace with a stone flag flying from the roof. There were two stone cheetahs outside with a stone ball, and a pretty little stone child, who had obviously been playing with them. In the courtyard of the palace was a stone fountain, some stone guards, and a stone rabbit caught in the act of eating some stone lettuce. It was all rather upsetting. Upstairs, in the stone banqueting hall, sat lots and lots of stone people around a stone table heaped with the most wonderful food imaginable, jellies and trifles and roast chickens and cream buns, but all made of – guess what.

"They must have offended an enchantress," said Jasleth knowingly. He could just imagine it – they had forgotten to ask her to the king's birthday feast, or perhaps it had been the little child's birthday, or the rabbit's. Anyway, in she had come with her winged chariot drawn by serpents, and changed everybody and everything into stone. He began to think that maybe King Minus had been lucky after all.

After they had been wandering round the banqueting hall for some time in bewilderment, Jasleth picked up one of the stone cream buns. Now a very strange thing happened. As he touched it, the bun appeared to change. Instead of grey stone, it seemed to become light-goldeny, rather crisp on the outside but full of jam and cream inside; just asking to be eaten. Jasleth couldn't resist putting it to his mouth.

"I bet it still tastes like stone," he thought, and took a bite. It didn't. It tasted like the nicest cream bun you could hope to taste. But no sooner had he bitten into it than –

"Jasleth!" cried Fearless in alarm.

Jasleth had changed into stone along with everything else.

You may wonder what it felt like to be changed into stone. It felt rather like being inside a stiff mound of ice-cold jelly. Jasleth found he couldn't move but he could still think, and the first thing he thought was:

"What an absolute fool I am! Now I shall never find my fortune. I'll be stuck here for the rest of my days, while Goodness ruins my father, and Prince Fearless gets back the Dragon Hoard without me," and believe it or not, two stone tears rolled out of Jasleth's stone eyes, and fell crash, bang, on to the floor.

However, Fearless still remembered that the enchanted raven had said he would not get back the Dragon Hoard unless Prince Jasleth was with him. He would never have left Jasleth behind. But it was a bit of a problem.

"I think we should ask the magic log what to do," decided Prince Fearless.

They all trooped out of the palace, through the wood, and down the beach to the ship. But when Fearless spoke to the log, he didn't get any answer.

The fact was that Maligna had been temporarily called away from her magic looking-glass. The toad, sniffling and coughing all the while, had packed its bags, and its bottles and eiderdowns and hankies, and said it was going home to its short-sighted auntie. It was better, the toad remarked, to be mistaken for a toadstool, than thrown into a pond when it was only trying to be pleasant.

"I'll turn you into a – " began Maligna furiously.

"Oh do you, won'd," snuffled the toad triumph-antly. "I've drung a whole boddle of your spell andidode. Whadever you do won'd have any affect ad all. And now good-snuffle-bye."

And it slammed the door.

All this was going on while Prince Fearless was entreating the magic log to speak to him, and just as Maligna was rushing back to the looking-glass, Fear-less was turning sorrowfully away.

"I'm afraid we shall have to think this one out for ourselves," he said sadly, not realising how jolly lucky they were that the log hadn't answered.

"Well," said Prince Onga, "I know a little magic myself. Back home I had a guardian genie. Perhaps I can conjure him up, and ask his advice."

Prince Sillius, who was frightened, said he would go back to the palace and keep guard over the stone Jasleth to make sure nobody hurt it. Fearless said he thought this was a very good idea.

When Prince Sillius arrived back in the banqueting hall, however, he had a bit of a shock. When he came in, there was Prince Jasleth, all stone, holding the stone bun, but when he looked again, Jasleth had vanished. There was a small stone raven stand-ing on the floor about where Jasleth had been, it is true, but Sillius didn't pay any attention to that.

"Jasleth, where are you?" he shouted, and went searching all over the palace. He felt he couldn't go back and tell Prince Fearless that he had lost Jasleth after just promising to guard him.

Jasleth, who had changed into a raven again, felt

70

even funnier as a stone raven than as a stone prince, although he didn't care for either very much.

Back on the beach, Prince Onga had made a little fire, and was throwing in various coloured powders from a pouch at his belt. They made everybody else cough. Lastly, he pulled a bright yellow feather from his headdress and threw that in also. There was a loud sizzling sound, and suddenly, up from the flames, shot a large genie. Its skin was like polished ebony, and it had long red hair. There were gold armlets all up its muscular arms, and a little bone through its nose. It looked very grand and a little fierce, but when it saw Prince Onga it smiled a big smile.

"Nice to see you again, little Onga," said the genie. It could say this because it was ten feet tall.

"Likewise, Lord Genie," said Prince Onga. "I'd like to introduce Prince Fearless."

Prince Fearless came forward bravely and shook the genie's hand. It was rather like shaking hands with a flash of lightning: hot and cold all at once, and full of little electric shocks.

"Now," said the genie, "what can I do for you?"

Prince Onga explained calmly and carefully all about Prince Jasleth and the stone bun, and when he had finished, the genie threw back its head and roared with laughter. It was the most alarming laugh. If you can imagine a thunderstorm laughing, that would be just right.

"Ah, yes," it said at last. "Well, I can tell you what happened. You see, this island was made stone by a special kind of thought-magic. When your Prince Jasleth picked up the stone bun, I expect he thought it was rather like a real cream bun, and the more he thought it, the more real it got. When he bit into it the magic went down inside him, and there he was, a stone like all the rest. But I'll give you some magic powder. Whatever you put it on will turn back into a real thing again."

It produced a big red box from the air, and handed it to Onga. Then, with another huge laugh, it said:

"I should imagine this will be a very nice little island when it's back to normal. I might stay here for a few hundred years – for a holiday."

Fearless and Onga and the other rowers all gathered handfuls of the magic powder, and threw it over everything in sight. The genie helped to spread it by blowing, but created such a gale that they had to ask it, tactfully, to stop. Gradually the sand turned golden and scattery, and the grass turned green, and the trees grew bark and moss and leaves, and the waterfall splashed and the stream gurgled, and all the little stone birds and animals started twittering and squeaking and howling and squawking, and tried out their wings, and blew on their paws, bit into their oranges, and fell off the branches in surprise.

The palace in the wood turned into crystal and silver, and the guards started marching in the court-yard, and the child and the cheetahs rolled over and over, and the rabbit bit a great chunk out of its lettuce. In all the rooms there was a bustling and a chattering, and from the kitchens a clatter of plates and pots, and a sizzling and crackling of ovens, and a smell of new bread. As the magic powder spread all over the island, the noise was incredible.

When Prince Fearless and Prince Onga went into the banqueting hall, they threw the powder along the table, and all the guests came alive in their splendid robes, and all the food turned into real food, so that the rowers' mouths watered. Last of all, Prince Jasleth, who, of course, had long since changed into a stone prince again, was given a good powder, and threw the stone bun in the air for joy.

In the middle of all the rejoicing, Prince Sillius came rushing in. He had had an awful job getting back to the banqueting hall, as there were people all over the place, laughing and exclaiming and getting in his way.

"Fearless!" he screamed. "I've lost Jasleth! I can't find him anywhere! I left him right here, went to look out of the window, and when I turned round – "

Jasleth went up and tried to explain that everything was all right now. Sillius grabbed his arm, and began to tell him as well.

When Sillius at last realised who it was, they had to sit him in a chair, and give him jelly to revive him.

Naturally, the king of the island was very grateful. He made the rowers stay with him for several days, giving them wonderful things to eat and drink, and lots of handsome clothes besides. He also made friends with the genie, and said it was to stay as long as it liked.

Even Jasleth was all right, as he always managed to change into a raven when there was nobody about.

Eventually Prince Fearless said thank you, but they really must be getting on, and did the king know anything about the Dragon Hoard? The king said oh yes, most certainly, and did they know they were going in the wrong direction to get there?

He gave them lots of careful instructions, and a huge farewell feast to see them off.

Just before everybody went to bed, he drew Onga and Jasleth and Fearless aside.

"I've got something to show you," he said, and winked.

He took a lamp, and led them up lots and lots of stairs to the very top of his palace. Soon the stairs stopped being marble and became stone, and everything else became stone too. It appeared that the top of this tower was so high that the magic powder hadn't blown up there.

The king led them out on to a balcony and what should they see there but a stone winged chariot drawn by stone winged serpents, and, in the chariot, stone hair flying, a bad-tempered-looking enchantress, all stone too.

"It seems," chuckled the king, "she was caught by her own spell, before she could get away, and, as the magic powder never reached her, she'll always be like this."

"It serves her right," said Jasleth with feeling.

"Well, it seems naughty to be pleased," said the king. "But she'd only be doing more mischief if she could."

Maligna, furious again, had watched all this. The minute she saw the stone enchantress she gave a scream, for it was another of her nasty friends who'd been at horrible witch-school with her. She couldn't count the times they had made evil-jam together.

Maligna would have liked to go straight away to the island, and make her into a real beastly enchant-

ress again, but she didn't dare while the genie was still there. She realised that the genie was a very powerful gentleman.

"I'll get even with you!" yelled Maligna, pointing at Jasleth in the looking-glass. "Just you wait and see!"

And she threw something at the toad, forgetting that it wasn't there any more.

CHAPTER FIVE

In which Awful is told a long, long story

After leaving the Stone Island behind, *The Quest*
sailed on for several uneventful and pleasant days,
across a peaceful sea. The water was so clear you
could see fish, like long pearls and pieces of coral,
swimming around under the surface. They even
passed a mermaid, doing just the right thing for once:
combing her long green curls and singing a sweet song
while a porpoise on a nearby rock accompanied her
by drumming on its belly with its flippers.

They did go by an island one day, whose king came
out in a rowing boat to tell them how handsome and
brave they all looked, and beg them to rescue his
people from a dreadful sea-monster. At dusk the
people left it food to stop it coming up the beach and
eating them, then ran away and hid. Now they had
nothing left to eat themselves, and were afraid the
monster would make short work of them when it
found they hadn't got it any supper. There was just
enough left for one night, so they had piled it all up on
the beach by the sea's edge.

Jasleth and Fearless and Onga and one or two other
brave rowers hid behind the rocks on the sea-shore
with their swords drawn. When the moon came up like
a silver lamp over the sea, a greenish scaly thing came

crawling up the beach. It wasn't very large, but it had five heads and lots of feet, and Jasleth began to wish he had stayed on the ship, or, better still, never left home.

"Who's going to rush out and smite it first?" whispered Prince Fearless nervously.

"Oh, you," said Prince Jasleth. "I wouldn't dream of dashing in ahead of you. I couldn't be so rude."

"Perhaps Onga would like the first try," suggested Fearless. Onga, however, wouldn't. While they were still arguing in hisses and whispers, Jasleth noticed that the sea-monster, instead of tucking into all the food, had sat down on the beach in front of it, and was crying. Tears ran down its ten cheeks, and sometimes it looked up at the moon and howled mournfully.

"It's working up a rage," said Prince Fearless.

Jasleth, however, wasn't so sure. He was remembering the monster-pet he had offered to slay at the start of his adventures. The sea-monster looked so miserable, Jasleth began to feel really sorry for it. So he crept out from his rock, and, gripping his sword very hard just in case, he went up to it.

"Excuse me!" called Jasleth.

Four of the heads went on crying. The other head peered down at him in surprise.

"Excuse me," repeated Jasleth. "But is anything wrong?"

"Wrong?" asked the first head.

"Wrong?"

"Wrong?"

"Wrong?"

"Wrong?" asked the other four, one after the other.

"Well," said Jasleth, "you seemed upset."

"Upset!" cried the monster in indignant voices. "You'd be upset if you'd been eating the muck those silly people put out for me – hunks of beef, potatoes, oranges – ugh!"

"Well," said Jasleth, "they gave you all that to stop you eating *them*."

"Eating *them*?" The monster almost laughed. "What a repulsive idea!"

"Then why have you been coming up on the beach every night?" asked Jasleth.

"I'll tell you," said the monster. "I'd have told them," and he pointed at the town on the hill, "if they'd stopped to listen. I only eat seaweed. That's all. Nothing else. Not all those horrible bits of meat and trifle and pies and stuff. I had a seaweed patch on the sea bottom, but my brother came out for the weekend, and ate it all up. Over there, just under the town walls, there's a beautiful lot of seaweed, just ripe, and so, so lovely." The monster looked hungrily up at it. "But every night, when I come out of the water to get it, what do I find but great wagons of beef, and jars of treacle piled all over the place, and I have to eat my way through them to get to my beautiful seaweed, and then, when I've eaten my way through, I feel so ill, all I can do is go back into the sea and lie down. And it never stops. Here it all is again. See those horrible pastries, and plates of mutton, and lemonade, and – and –" and it burst into fresh tears.

Jasleth went round the rocks and told the others. At first they didn't believe him. When he had finally convinced them all, they came out, and helped the

78

monster push the food to one side. It hadn't been strong enough to do it on its own. Then it went galloping up the hill, and sat down in the seaweed and gobbled and gobbled.

The people in the town didn't believe Jasleth either. When they saw the monster charging up the hill towards them, they thought it had come to eat them, and ran out, yelling, into the forest. When the prince at last persuaded them to come back, they found the monster lying happily on its back, with all its legs in the air, purring softly to itself.

"Lovely seaweed," it kept murmuring. "Lovely, *lovely* seaweed."

The people decided to plant the beach with seaweed to keep the monster happy. They soon stopped being afraid of it, and it used to take the children for rides, and help sell ices on hot days by revolving all its heads like a fan to keep them cool.

"Of course," said Fearless, as *The Quest* sailed off, "just as well we spotted the poor thing crying in time, before I chopped its heads off with one blow."

Because everything had gone so well, they hadn't thought to ask the magic log for any advice.

As for Maligna, she had been running around for days, trying to conjure up storms and gales, but, luckily for *The Quest*, the toad had made a mess of everything before it left, just to show her. It had put all the herbs and horrors in the wrong jars, and stirred them up with bats-balm and rats-ruin, and then stuck the wrong labels on them. Maligna was having a dreadful time. Whenever she threw anything into the cauldron there was a loud explosion that blew her nearly out of the window. You can imagine what her temper was like.

The new postman was trudging up the mountain one day when he was rather surprised to find his arms full of two trembling black wolves, feebly yelping:

"Help! Help! The enchantress is after us! We never meant to bite anybody! Please save us, nice kind Mr Postman!" and licking his face with their big black tongues.

"There, there, doggies," soothed the postman, put them down, and ran for his life. Feebly yelping or not, he knew a wolf when he saw one.

Not long after this, just as Maligna was putting her poor bats up in curlers, she saw something in the magic looking-glass that made her feel a lot better. *The Quest* was sailing towards a strip of land where another nasty friend of Maligna's lived. It was a mad old wizard called Awful. He had a long white beard, and long white hair, and wore three pairs of glasses at once. Looking at him, you might have thought that he was just a dear potty old gentleman, but if you were unfortunate enough to be invited into his palace, you soon found out he wasn't.

Fearless was walking up the deck to the figure-head.

"Excuse me, oh magic log," began Fearless.

"Yes, my dear," screeched Maligna excitedly, and in a hurry, and not a bit sweetly.

Fearless looked rather surprised, but he said:

"We were wondering if that bit of land over there was a good place to put in to. We'd like to take in some fresh fruit and –"

80

"Yes! Yes!" cried Maligna. "Just the place! Couldn't be better! Miles of fruit trees everywhere!"

"Oh – er – thank you," said Fearless, almost speechless at her enthusiasm. He went back and told everyone what a wonderful place they had come to, and what luck it was to be there.

Awful had already seen the ship through his spyglass, and was dancing delightedly into his banqueting hall.

"Guests! Guests!" he shrilled, and gave an old demon, asleep on the table, a dreadful prod in the ribs to wake him up. "Orders! Orders!" yelled Awful. "Write it down, write it down at once! And don't leave anything out or I shall tie your tail to the ironing board!"

The demon grumbled, and put its notebook on the floor. Then it stood on its hands and wrote with one of its horns, which it dipped in the inkwell beforehand. It made a lot of blots.

"What a messer you are!" cried the wizard. "Never mind! Never mind! Write this down! Half a ton of venison, twenty roast geese, forty honey puddings and ten barrels of cider. I want the best gold plates out, and tell those glow-worms to be in the lamps by four o'clock sharp. The last one in will be changed into a purple dandelion! Underline that! Now! Now!" Awful brushed several layers of dust off the table with his beard and shook it out like a duster all over the demon. "Go and kick those snakes awake! And the cook!" The cook was an old nanny-goat. "And tell that monster in the cellar that if it doesn't heat up the cauldron piping hot tonight, I'll throw it upstairs."

Prince Fearless and the rowers, meanwhile, had come ashore. Fearless was looking round him in puzzlement.

"You know," he confided to Jasleth, "I don't see a single fruit tree anywhere."

"No," said Jasleth. "But there's a big black palace up there, with red glass windows."

"So there is," agreed Fearless.

At this moment, there was a squeaky, croaky sort of fanfare, and out of the palace came trooping a lot of miserable-looking snakes in tight black uniforms.

"Welcome," cried the first snake, who was wearing the tightest uniform, "to our master's home."

"Thank you," said Fearless.

"Our master," gasped the snake, "hopes that you will join him for his evening feast."

"That's very kind," said Jasleth. "Who is your master?"

"All-fluff-um-puff," mumbled the snake. Obviously, the name "Awful" might be a bit off-putting to some people.

"Who?" asked Fearless.

"Puff-um-fluff-huff," gasped the snake, and went down to the beach to mop its flushed face with some cool sea-water.

"Oh, well," said Fearless. "It would be rude to refuse."

He had already caught the delicious smell of honey pudding.

The snakes led them up to the palace door, and took them inside.

When they entered the banqueting hall, they were rather surprised. The pillars were made of solid gold,

but were dim with grime and had festoons of cobwebs
hanging between them. On the table were golden
dishes heaped with lovely food but two funny-looking
persons with long tails and horns and little hooves
were lying about in the middle of it all, playing skittles
with the salt-cellars and an orange.

Just then a dear old gentleman with a long beard
and three pairs of glasses popped into the room.

"Welcome! Welcome!" he cried. Then, "Get off!
Get off!" and with a lash of his beard he swatted the
two demons off the table. "Please be seated," invited
the wizard. "And do help yourselves."

Everybody sat down, and did just that. They were all very hungry and the food was gorgeous.

Apart from the food, however, it was an odd sort of feast. First of all, the glow-worms in the lamps kept falling asleep, and, when they did so, their lights went out and that part of the room became so dark that everyone started eating each other's dinner by mistake. Whenever this happened the wizard would rush screaming across the hall and bang on the lamp with his stick until the light came on again.

Then there was the orchestra.

There were three sullen crocodiles with harps, and a fed-up-looking alligator with a small drum. The noise they made gave Prince Jasleth a headache. And if this weren't enough, various demons and monsters kept playfully bounding on to and across the table, throwing pudding at each other. Each time they did, the wizard would shriek at them and they would run off, but not for long. At one point a nanny-goat in an apron came through the door and said it was sick and tired of people always racing about in its kitchen and one monster had fallen in the soup and it was giving in its notice.

When the rowers were very full, and were starting to think up excuses to leave, the wizard banged on the table, the ghastly orchestra stopped playing, and a couple of lamps, that were just nodding off, woke up with a start.

"Now it's time for the party games!" cried Awful, gleefully.

"Oh, er – well – " began Prince Fearless.

"You see – " said Jasleth.

84

"The first game," chortled the wizard, "is called 'See who can get up from his chair first'."

Fearless thought that this was a splendid game, and so did everyone else. But the minute they tried to get up, they found that something very unpleasant had happened. They were all stuck fast. It wasn't like being stuck with glue, it was as if they had grown into their chairs, and the chairs were fastened to the floor.

"Ha! Ha!" shouted the wizard. "Can't get up, after all! It's magic, my boys, that's what it is! You can't get up till I let you, and I *won't* let you. Now I'm going to tell you about the second party game. The second party game is the one I play with all the travellers who stop off at my palace. It's called 'One of you will now tell me a story, or else I'll open a trap door beneath your chair, and you'll fall into a big hot cauldron underneath'!"

Everyone was horrified. They had no doubt at all that the wizard would do just that, and there was absolutely no need for him to open the door under an empty chair in order to prove it to them. He did, though, and there *was* a cauldron, all steaming and bubbling, obviously full of the nastiest things you could imagine, and altogether thoroughly horrid.

"It's all very fair, you see," said the wizard happily. "Just as long as one of you keeps telling a story the magic door won't open, but the minute you run out of ideas – Plop! Sizzle! Swoosh! Choose whoever you like to tell the story; I don't mind," Awful added generously. "But hurry up, or I'll throw you in any-way!"

Everyone was still sitting staring at each other,

when Jasleth suddenly thought of a way they might do it. So he sat up straight and began.

"Once upon a time," said Jasleth, just saying the first things that came into his head, "there was a beautiful young princess called Soppy. Soppy lived in a golden palace with her father and mother and a lot of chickens. You may wonder why the chickens lived in the palace with the king and queen, but I might as well tell you that the chickens used to wonder why the king and queen lived in the palace with *them*. Anyway, one day, as Soppy and the chickens were walking through the palace garden, what should they see but a – " Here Prince Jasleth broke off, and tapped Onga on the arm.

"Your turn!" he hissed.

It didn't take Onga more than half a second to get the idea. He carried on right where Jasleth had left off, also saying the first things that came into his head.

"What should they see," purred Onga, "but an enormous elephant, holding a rose in its trunk. 'For you, lovely Soppy,' cried the elephant, giving Soppy the rose. 'Had I but realised, I would have brought something for your chickens as well.' – 'That's all right,' said Soppy. 'But perhaps you could give us all a ride on your back?' The elephant lifted up Soppy and the chickens, but no sooner had it taken a step towards the garden gate, than – " Onga tapped Fearless on the shoulder, and Fearless was all ready.

"Than an enormous dragon came flying into the garden, and seized Soppy in its talons and flew off with her. Soppy wept, and begged the dragon to put her down, but the dragon only laughed. Soon they arrived at his big dark cave, and flew in. 'Now,' cried the dragon, cruelly, 'I shall eat you up!'" Suddenly, seeing the possible end of the story, Fearless broke off, and looked worried, but the fourth rower was waiting to go on, and continued:

"'Please don't eat me!' begged Soppy. 'I'm very clever, and can spin cobwebs into gold!' and so saying, Soppy dragged down a couple of tons of cobwebs, and began to spin them all over the place. The dragon, who was allergic to gold, came out in an awful rash, and asked her to leave at once. This Soppy gladly did, but she didn't know where she was. All around were dark woods and strange mountains. Soppy sat down and wept. 'Who will help me?' wept Soppy."

" 'I will!' cried a tiny voice," went on the fifth rower. "And what should she see, sitting on the grass, but a three-headed grass-snake. Soppy jumped up and screamed with fright. 'Do not fear!' cried the grass-snake. 'I am really a handsome prince under a spell. If you kiss me on top of the head, I will turn back into my former shape.' Soppy picked up the snake, and tenderly kissed its three heads, one after the other – and then – "

"And then," said the sixth rower, "the snake screamed with laughter, and ran away. 'Fooled you that time!' it yelled. Meanwhile – "

"Meanwhile, the elephant, who was *really* an enchanted prince," said the seventh rower, "was running around, trying to find out where the dragon lived, so that it could go and rescue Soppy. Nobody seemed to know, however, so the elephant set out to find her on its own. It walked and walked, and it got blisters. 'I wish – ' said the elephant – "

" 'I wish,' " said the eighth rower, " 'I had never started on this stupid business.' It sat down under a shady tree, and ate its peanut sandwiches. Suddenly a little man popped up from behind a rock. He was wearing a scarlet hat, and carried a magic wand. 'I will grant you three wishes,' cried the little man. 'Good,' said the elephant prince. 'Then first of all, I wish for a –' "

" 'For another sandwich,' " said the ninth rower. " 'Secondly, I wish for –' "

" 'For a strawberry ice,' " said the tenth. " 'And thirdly –' "

" 'For a chocolate eclair –' " said the eleventh.

" 'What a silly elephant you are!' said the little man," said the twelfth rower. " 'You've forgotten all about Soppy!' – "

" 'No I haven't,' " said the thirteenth, " 'but I was hungry.' 'There you are, then,' said the little man, and vanished. When the elephant had finished its sandwiches and ice and eclair, it went on with its journey. It travelled for many days until one morning, what should it see but – "

"But a big dark cave in the mountainside," went on the fourteenth rower. "So the elephant squeezed in, and, right at the back, he saw the dragon, surrounded by medicine bottles, scratching and complaining. It had still got its nasty itchy rash from the gold. 'Pardon me,' said the elephant. 'Why, what have you done?' cried the dragon."

" 'I came to ask,' said the elephant, 'where the Princess Soppy is,' " said the fifteenth rower. " 'Oh,' said the dragon, 'She is –' "

" ' She's gone,' " said the sixteenth. " 'I was going

to eat her, but she kept on talking about cobwebs, and spinning gold, so I asked her to leave. I think she must be in the forest somewhere.' "

"Sure enough," went on the seventeenth rower, "Soppy was still wandering around in the forest, weeping bitterly, and spinning the odd cobweb into gold here and there to try to keep her spirits up. 'I wish a handsome prince would come and rescue me,' wept Soppy. Just then –"

"Just then," said the eighteenth rower, "a handsome prince rode by on a white charger. 'Oh! At last!' cried Soppy. 'Have you come to rescue me?' 'I'm sorry,' said the prince. 'I have eight rescues to carry out already and I'm late as it is. Perhaps next year –' Soppy was very upset. She sat down on the grass, and soon cried herself to sleep. Meanwhile –"

"Meanwhile," went on the nineteenth rower, "a wicked enchanter called All-Fluffumpuff" (and the nineteenth rower looked straight at Awful) "had seen Soppy spinning all the cobwebs into gold. His palace was full of cobwebs" (and the nineteenth rower looked all round at the cobwebs swaying from the pillars), "and he thought it would be fine to make them prettier."

"So," said the twentieth rower, "he flew down in his bat-chariot, and carried Soppy off to his palace by the sea-shore."

" 'Help!' screamed Soppy," screamed the twenty-first rower.

" 'Help! Help!' " scream-added the twenty-second.

"But it was no use," continued the twenty-third. " 'Here we are!' cried the horrible wizard, and there they were."

"Soppy span as many cobwebs as she could into gold," went on the twenty-fourth rower. "She thought the sooner she finished them, the sooner the wizard would let her go, and, after all, he might always get a rash. Every day, when her work was finished, she would go to the palace windows, and look out in all directions to see if her prince was coming, but he never was. One day, however –"

"One day, a little old woman stopped at the palace," said the twenty-fifth rower. "She was selling gold polish. Soppy went down and told the little old woman all her troubles. 'What a nasty old wizard he is, to be sure,' said the little old woman. 'I hope he falls into one of his own cauldrons!'"

As you can see, the story had now got half-way round the table, and, as you can guess, the wizard was very angry. To begin with, no one was having any trouble thinking up ideas; in fact, they all seemed to be enjoying themselves rather a lot. Secondly, Awful didn't like the way they kept on talking about the "nasty old wizard". He'd certainly never given a feast like this before.

" 'I was hoping a prince would come and rescue me,' " the twenty-sixth rower was going on.

Awful jumped up.

"Down you all go into the cauldron!" he yelled.

But as the story was still in full swing, the magic doors wouldn't work. Awful jumped up and down in rage, and his beard fell into the gravy.

" 'Well, dear,' said the little old woman," said the twenty-seventh rower. " 'Here is a magic honey pot. Whoever eats any of the honey will turn into a bee, or a wasp, I forget which.' "

" 'Oh, thank you!' said Soppy," said the eighth rower.

"Stop it at once!" yelled the wizard, shaking gravy everywhere.

But they wouldn't. The twenty-ninth and thirtieth and thirty-first rowers went on to say how Soppy gave the wizard the honey, and he turned into a butterfly. (The thirtieth rower had forgotten that it was supposed to be a wasp or a bee, but the thirty-first hadn't, and made the butterfly go round, buzzing loudly.) Once this was done, Soppy ran away from the palace into the woods, where she was chased by a large brown bull called Darling. The thirty-second, thirty-third, thirty-fourth, thirty-fifth and thirty-sixth rowers explained how a porcupine obligingly tripped up the bull, which fell over and hurt its leg. Soppy was so sorry for it that she bound up its hoof, and then found out that the bull was really a good fairy under a spell, who promptly granted her anything she wished for.

The thirty-seventh said Soppy wished for a piece of toast and marmalade, but the thirty-eighth rower said that the good fairy was so pleased at this simple request that she granted her another, and this time Soppy wished for her prince.

The thirty-ninth, fortieth, forty-first, forty-second, forty-third, forty-fourth and forty-fifth rowers told how the elephant then came galloping into the wood, and said he had come to rescue her. Soppy burst into tears, and the elephant had to explain that he was really a prince, and that to break the spell cast over him Soppy would have to fetch a silver rose from a magic rose-garden somewhere or other.

The forty-sixth, forty-seventh, forty-eighth and forty-ninth rowers said Soppy went to get the rose, on which she pricked her finger and became an enchanted tree. The elephant, however, had followed her, and, on sniffing the silver rose, turned into a handsome prince, and changed Soppy back again by kissing one of her branches.

All this time, the wizard had been running round the table, yelling and interrupting, or trying to, and threatening all sorts of awful things, none of which he could do because he was in such a state he had forgotten the right spells.

When it got to the fiftieth rower, Awful was very relieved. He thought this would be the end of the dreadful story.

"That, however," said the fiftieth rower, "was only the adventure of the elephant prince and Princess Soppy. Now we come to the exciting tale of their daughter, Princess Silly – "

Whereupon Jasleth, the first rower, who started everything, gave a broad smile, and continued:

"Princess Silly had golden hair and an aunt called Horrid. Horrid was a bad enchantress, and one day – (your turn, Onga) – "

At this, and seeing that Onga was all ready to begin again, as all the others appeared to be, too, Awful gave a piercing screech, and fled from the hall, scattering demons and snakes on every side.

He jumped into his bat-chariot, and thrashed his whip, and was soon flying across the night sky, shaking his fist and his gravy-stained beard at the moon.

"I'm never going back!" cried Awful. "Never! Never! The shame! Outwitted! Outwitted!"

Then the rowers suddenly found that they could move from their chairs. They also found all sorts of marvellous treasure: great cupboards full of gold and heaps of precious gems, rubies and emeralds and pearls, not to mention spell-books full of useful spells, and magic potions that would be sure to come in handy.

All the demons and snakes and crocodiles and everyone else seemed delighted that Awful had gone – and they could all play skittles on the banqueting table. They loaded *The Quest* with gold and jewels, and begged the rowers to write and let them know how they got on in the land of the Dragon Hoard.

"Onga," Jasleth asked, as they pulled at their oars again under the moon, "what *did* Horrid do?"

"Oh, well," began Onga.

They went on telling the story for days.

CHAPTER SIX

In which Maligna sprinkles Sea-Wickedness, and
The Quest *goes to the sea-bottom*

Once everyone had got over the excitement of the
adventure with Awful, the rowers began to remember
that it was the magic log that had said what a wonderful place to land the wizard's beach would be. As it
had turned out, everything had been for the best, but
if they hadn't told their story so well they might all
have ended up in Awful's awful cauldron. Several of
the rowers were for going up to the log and giving it
a piece of their minds. Prince Fearless, however,
always romantic and gallant, said the magic log was
a lady and they mustn't upset it.

He did go up himself, one afternoon, and say that
perhaps it had been mistaken in telling them the
wizard's beach had lots of fruit trees. He added that
the log wasn't to worry, but they *had* very nearly
finished their quest in a cauldron.

"Worry!" screamed the log's voice angrily. Fearless jumped back a yard or so in alarm. "Pah! It
would have done you good!"

Fearless went and told Jasleth in private.

"Well," said Jasleth, "I've suspected for some time
that that log isn't on our side. Ever since it sent us in
the wrong direction, in fact. I've been trying to think
of some way to test it."

"Is that why you keep disappearing for odd hours every day?" asked Fearless.

"Oh – er – yes," said Jasleth, "that's right."

"And have you thought of any plan?"

"Oh – er – no," said Jasleth.

It was hardly surprising that Maligna was in a bad temper. All her horrible tricks had come to nothing, and Jasleth and the others were doing splendidly. She couldn't think what to do next, so she tied all the bats up in black ribbons, glued Sweetie's and Poppet's tails together, and wrote a beastly letter to the toad's auntie who was so short-sighted that she couldn't read it anyway.

Eventually she peeped into her magic looking-glass, and saw that *The Quest* was sailing over one of the most important sea kingdoms. Down through the cool green currents, on a throne of coral in a palace of conch-shells and pearls, sat a very grand mermaid called Queen Emeraldis. Now there was one spell potion that the toad hadn't got at to make a mess of, and that was a bottle of something called Sea-Wickedness. It was a decoction of special seaweeds and sea-shells, and enchanters had been using it for a long time to cause trouble under the sea. A few drops were enough to cause the most sedate mermaid or fish to become giggly and very badly behaved.

Here was Maligna's chance.

She seized the bottle of Sea-Wickedness, and threw her magic dust over herself so that she vanished from her palace and reappeared, hovering a few feet over the sea, in mid-air. She could see *The Quest* sailing towards her, so she simply uncorked the bottle and threw it into the water. Down and down it sank, the Sea-Wickedness running out as it went.

"Now just you wait and see, dear Jasleth!" cried Maligna happily, and hurriedly disappeared back to her palace again.

Soon everybody on the sea-bed was in high spirits and behaving very badly indeed. The mermen, who lived in little white coral cottages among the seaweed forests, began to pick up oysters and throw them at each other. The whales began to dance wildly around, shouting at the tops of their voices and wearing silly party hats made of anemones. Queen Emeraldis, herself, shook out her emerald-green hair and joined her terrapins in chasing a sea-serpent all over the palace, until it finally tied itself up into a knot round one of the pillars and refused to be chased any more.

It wasn't long before one of the mermaids spotted *The Quest* sailing overhead, her oars churning up the water.

"Queen Emeraldis!" she cried. "Let's bring those silly mortals down here to play with us. We can hang our magic sea-shells round their necks so they can breathe under water as we do, and we can have oh-so-much fun with their nice big ship."

"Why, what a good idea!" laughed Emeraldis.

She got into her chariot, which was made out of a huge pear-shaped pink shell, drawn by six silver sea-horses, and set her crown on her long green hair.

"Up we go!" she cried, and her six sea-horses waved their fins. Up, up, up they went, through showers of bubbles and ferns, while the light got brighter and brighter, until suddenly the chariot

broke the surface of the water and rose on a big wave just in front of the prow of *The Quest*.

"Look out!" yelled Sillius, who was the look out that day. "An enormous mermaid right ahead of us. Help!"

Emeraldis didn't like people saying she was enormous. She was only nine feet tall, which, for a queen mermaid, was quite tiny.

"Halt!" she ordered.

The rowers stopped rowing, and, as there wasn't much wind, *The Quest* slowed right down just beside Queen Emeraldis' chariot.

"I," announced Emeraldis, "am the queen mermaid of Emerald Kingdom. I command you to come to the sea-bottom to run races with the terrapins, and let us play with your ship," and she giggled.

Prince Fearless, gallant as usual, but also quite worried, bowed to her and said:

"Beautiful madam, er – hem, we'd love to come down to the sea-bottom, but – er – we really have to get on. Thank you, anyway. I hope the terrapins won't be too disappointed."

"Seize them!" yelled Emeraldis.

Immediately several hundred anemones stuck themselves to the underside of the ship, and attached to the anemones were long ropes of strong plaited seaweed. All the mermen and mermaids and whales and dolphins pulled hard, and –

"Help!" screamed Sillius. "We're sinking!"

"We must keep calm," said Fearless, gnawing his fingernails.

"Surely you needn't do this," Onga said reasonably to Emeraldis. "We could always visit you on the way back."

"No good!" howled Emeraldis. "No good at all!"

Down went the prow with a sort of creaky groan, and the ship filled up with water. It didn't take long after that. Some of the rowers tried to swim away, but Emeraldis' octopuses grabbed them, and the sharks threatened to bite them if they didn't do as Queen Emeraldis commanded. So they did.

As soon as they were all in the sea, an old skate came up and hung the magic sea-shells around their necks which meant they could breathe under water, and it really was beautiful, going down. The water changed colour, getting darker and darker green, with little bubbles floating by in it like silver butterflies. There were great forests of dark blue and scarlet seaweed, full of fish swimming around like birds flying through a forest at twilight.

Eventually they reached Queen Emeraldis' palace, and *The Quest* came to rest on the pale sand. At once the mermaids and mermen and everyone else began to swim all over it, taking out the supplies and throwing them about, and dressing up in the jewels that had come from Awful's palace. Meanwhile, Queen Emeraldis made the questors run races with the terrapins, skip octopus-tentacles, and play football with the mermen, all of which was very tiring indeed, and not much fun as the terrapins and mermen always won.

Jasleth and Onga and Fearless and the others were soon worn out. They sat down on the sand.

"Come along!" cried Queen Emeraldis. "More games! More games!"

The questors looked at each other, and eventually Fearless stood up and said:

"I'm sorry, your majesty, but we refuse."

"Refuse?" Emeraldis was very surprised. Then she remembered she was a queen, and shouted, "Throw them into the dungeons!"

As dungeons go, Emeraldis' dungeons were rather nice. They were big green caves, full of shells and ferns, and fish swam in and out of small holes in the cave-sides. The holes, however, were the only way out once the big conch-shell door had been locked on them, and none of the rowers was anything like small enough to get out through a hole that size.

"If only we could get to *The Quest*," said Jasleth,

"I'm sure one of those spell-books of Awful's would help us find a way to escape. As it is, Onga can't even talk to his genie."

"No," said Onga. "I need a fire for that, and, anyway, one of the mermaids took my headdress with the magic feathers."

"I suppose we'll just have to make the best of it," said Jasleth.

And then it happened.

Up till now, Jasleth had managed to get away with changing into a raven every day. Either he had been somewhere out of sight, or else nobody had been looking. With fifty young men on a ship, one more or less wasn't that easy to notice. But this time Jasleth had just spoken, and everyone was looking at him, nodding in sad agreement, when – whoosh! There was Jasleth no longer. There, instead, was a black bird, looking rather guilty, and trying to get behind a shell and hide.

"Why, Jasleth," said Onga, in his velvety voice, "you've changed into a raven!"

"Shut up!" hissed the raven.

"Jasleth," said Fearless, "did you do it yourself, or did it just happen? Can you always do it?"

"No, no," said the raven nervously, hopping about. "It's not happened before."

"But what about those hours you are missing every day?" asked Fearless. "I often thought I saw a raven flying around then. Was it you?" And then, in sudden amazement, and in a dry cold voice, Fearless asked, "And was it you, in your raven shape, who flew into the market place, and said you were an enchanted sign?"

Jasleth longed for the sand to open up and swallow him, but, of course, it wouldn't. So, in a very humble voice, blushing hotly under his black feathers, Jasleth explained all about his father's kingdom, and Maligna's horrible birthday presents. How he had set off to seek his fortune to save his father from ruin, and the dreadful trouble that had befallen him and made him all muddy and torn, and how the trick of the enchanted raven had seemed the only way. When he had finished, he sat down on the shell and hung his head so that his beak touched his chest, and waited for Fearless to say how awful he was and how everything was his fault.

However, it was Onga who spoke first.

"Well," said Onga. "If I remember, the enchanted raven – that is you, Jasleth – told Fearless that the Quest wouldn't be successful unless you were on it."

"Yes," muttered Jasleth. "It was a dreadful lie, I know."

"Well," said Onga. "First of all, we couldn't have rescued all those people on the stone island if you hadn't been there to eat that cream bun and get changed into stone yourself. Secondly, we could never have got that muddle sorted out with the sea-monster who only wanted seaweed if you hadn't been brave and kind enough to go and ask it why it was crying. Thirdly, we should all be in Wizard Awful's cauldron by now if you hadn't started us off on that story."

Jasleth raised his raven head, and looked at Onga.

"Speaking for myself," said Onga, "I think that it's a very good thing that Jasleth came with us, and I don't think we'd have got this far without him. Apart from which, he did what he did, back in King

Purple's kingdom, not just for himself, but to help his family, which is surely a good enough excuse."

There was a moment of silence, and then all the other forty-eight rowers, including Prince Fearless, cheered and clapped, and shouted that they agreed, and Jasleth was such a jolly good fellow anyway, how could they do anything else but forgive him?

Jasleth was so pleased and relieved that he took to his wings, and flew round through the water, which made everyone clap and cheer even louder. He was in mid-flight when suddenly a fish bigger than he was swam in through a hole and knocked him over.

"Look!" said Jasleth. "I've got an idea! Now I'm small enough to get out of the dungeon through one of these holes, maybe I'm small enough to get on to the ship without being noticed. Supposing I go and have a look at Awful's spell-books, and see what I can find."

"Just as well you came with us, Jasleth," said Onga.

Everyone else agreed.

Jasleth got out through the hole with the greatest of ease, and made for *The Quest*. It was hardly recognisable, as it was festooned with anemones and ferns and seaweed and there were mermaids and porpoises swimming all over it.

He wondered if he might possibly pass for a fish, but decided he wouldn't. He was just thinking what to do, when he noticed a big creamy shell lying in the sand. There were two windows near its top. Jasleth got into it and found it fitted perfectly. Only his feet showed underneath, and his eyes were just the right height for him to be able to see through the windows. Anyone would have thought he was just a shell, aimlessly rolling towards *The Quest*.

He rolled on across the deck to the hatch, and went down into the hold.

What a mess there was down there! The mermaids had pulled open all the chests, and thrown food and clothing and the gold from Awful's palace all over the place. Eventually Jasleth found a spell-book under a side of bacon and a fur cloak. Luckily it had several pages entitled, *Spells For The Sea Folk*, and, yes, there was one called *A Spell To Put All Sea Things, Including Mermaids, Into A Deep Slumber*. On the very next page was another entitled *A Spell To Bring A Ship Up From The Sea-Bottom And Dry Her Out*.

No sooner read than done.

Jasleth went up on the deck, still looking like a shell, and read out the first spell to make all the sea things sleep. It was such a strong spell that Jasleth himself started yawning, and had to hop about to keep awake. As for the mermaids, their heads sank on their breasts, and they dropped the rubies and pearls and cheeses they had been holding, and slid quietly over the ship's side on to the soft sand. The dolphins smiled as they slept, and the porpoises let the sharks use their bellies as pillows. Even Queen Emeraldis lay asleep in her shell chariot, together with her sleeping sea-horses, one of whom had been eating Onga's headdress.

Jasleth took off his shell, hurried back to the dungeon, and opened the door with his beak. Everyone came flooding out, and soon they were all back in the ship. Even the anemones had fallen off into the sand,

and the ferns had unlooped from the mast, as if they, too, were asleep.

Jasleth quickly said the second spell, and everyone was delighted when *The Quest* gave a little shudder, and then began to lift. Up and up she went, up and up to where the light got clear and pale and bright and green, and soon the sun broke through on to their faces, and they were free.

The spell was also, as it said it was, good for drying the ship out, although for some days she was still a bit damp here and there.

As for the magic shells that had made them able to breathe under water, everyone wanted to keep them, but the moment the sun shone on them, they crumbled away into nothing.

"Oh well," said Jasleth, "it can't be helped," and changed back into a prince.

Everybody shook hands with him, and hugged him, and clapped him on the back, and said, thank goodness he had come with them, and wasn't he lucky, really, to be able to fly.

"Thank you," said Jasleth – and – "I'm glad I came, too" – and – "It's rather like swimming, almost."

Even the mermaids and dolphins, when they woke up, were glad the ship had gone away. The Sea-Wickedness had ebbed, and they were already beginning to feel ashamed. Queen Emeraldis wore a veil of lace-weed for a week to hide her blushes.

PART THREE
The Nasty Tasks

CHAPTER SEVEN

In which Princess Jadelli has a visitor,
Prince Jasleth tames two fierce horses, and the
palace pool goes into a jug

The weather remained calm and *The Quest* sailed on,
but Jasleth said they must settle the matter of the
magic log one way or another. Ever since their adventure with Queen Emeraldis, the questors had been
on the lookout for trouble. By using one of the spells in
Awful's book, they found out that they were coming
to some sharp rocks which would be dangerous to
sail near at night, so Fearless, as a test, went up to the
magic log and asked it if it would be safe for them to
sail on.

Now it happened that Maligna didn't know they
had Awful's spell-book. She had to leave the magic
looking-glass once in a while to make herself some
rank-weed sandwiches, and, since the toad had left,
there was nobody to watch in her place, except, of
course, Sweetie and Poppet, but she had shut them
up inside an oak tree yesterday, and then forgotten
about them. So when asked, she hastily swallowed her
sandwiches and cried, "Yes, yes! Fair weather and a
fathomless bottom," because she had seen the rocks
earlier on, and hoped *The Quest* would be wrecked on
them.

As the log had now told them to do what they knew to be the wrong thing, Jasleth said it proved it was not on their side. Fearless told the log just what he thought of it, and they took it off the prow and threw it overboard. Sillius even shook his fist at it as it floated away, but it was only a piece of driftwood really, so none of them need have bothered.

Maligna was now in a towering rage. She no longer had an excuse for talking to the rowers and giving them bad advice, and, as her spells were still in an awful mess, she couldn't conjure up any storms, or anything like that either. She watched helplessly as the ship sailed on over calm blue waters, having a few very mild adventures here and there, like rescuing a sea-serpent princess who had got caught up in some rather tough seaweed. Her father, a grey old serpent, gave them a big basket full of pearls to show how thankful he was.

And then, one morning, horror of horrors, Maligna saw the long dark outline of a new coast, and realised that *The Quest* was a day's journey away from the land of the Dragon Hoard.

She racked her brains. Then she remembered that King Pumble, the king who owned the Dragon Hoard at the moment, had a young daughter who had gone to witch-school and was learning to be an enchantress. Maligna at once let out Sweetie and Poppet, unglued their tails, and told them to go and fetch her a winged chariot drawn by fire-breathing serpents. Then she put on her best black robe that was embroidered all over with magic signs in gold and purple, and an enormous headdress with two horns sticking out of it, and a gold veil. Sweetie and Poppet had a lot of trouble getting the chariot as Maligna still hadn't paid her bill to Winged-Serpent Chariot Hire, but the old monster agreed to produce one once the two wolves had chased him up a tree and told him Maligna had forgotten to feed them for three days.

The chariot was the best he had, all gold with sapphires set in the sides, and the serpents were gold too, and breathed blue flames.

"This should impress that King's daughter," cried Maligna, and set off, only whipping the serpents lightly, so as not to take the sheen off their scales.

She arrived at King Pumble's palace just before sunset. She saw the King's daughter feeding some black swans in the royal gardens, and came crashing down among the poplar trees, setting some of the King's best grapevines on fire.

The princess turned, and when she saw that it was obviously a powerful and important enchantress, she gave a curtsey. Young enchantresses were always taught at witch-school to be respectful to their superiors and to listen to their advice.

"Good evening, my dear," said Maligna, in her most syrupy voice.

The princess was sixteen years old, and very beautiful. She was tall and slim, with a white skin, long black hair, and jade-green eyes. When Maligna used her syrupy voice, these eyes narrowed very slightly, and Maligna realised that the princess was no fool, and she would have to be clever. She had been hoping to find a witch as malignant as she was, but the princess wasn't a bit malignant. She had just attended witch-school to gain experience, and she had a kind heart and a quick mind.

"Well, now, my dear," said Maligna grandly, "what is your name?"

"I'm Princess Jadelli," said the princess. "Do please sit down, and I'll get you some tea."

"No, no, quite all right, my dear. I can't stop long, you know. I've come to warn you," said Maligna.

"Warn me of what?" asked the princess.

"Well, now," said Maligna, casually changing one of the poplar trees into solid silver, to impress Jadelli. "Soon a ship will sail into the harbour, and some strangers will come asking for the Dragon Hoard."

"Oh, *that*," said the princess. "Well, I expect Father will let them have it. He doesn't like it. He says it's too dangerous for us to have, and just leaves it where it is. Nobody's seen it for years. I've never seen it; I don't even know what it is, do you?"

"Ah," said Maligna. "My child, you must understand that the Dragon Hoard must stay where it is, and not be taken from your kingdom. If it goes, the kingdom's luck will go with it. Everybody will get measles and whooping cough, and there will be a drought and then a flood."

Jadelli looked rather alarmed.

"Pardon me, but are you sure?" she asked.

"My poor child, I'm afraid so. I saw it in my magic glass which foretells the future, and I came to warn you at once. Whatever you do, you mustn't let the strangers take the Dragon Hoard away."

"I see," said Jadelli, looking thoughtful. "And how shall I stop them? Father will want to give them the Dragon Hoard at once, to get rid of it."

"Where is the Hoard?" asked Maligna. "Is it guarded?"

"Oh, the usual sort of thing," said Jadelli. "It's in a magic grove of oak trees, guarded by a dragon."

"Oh, well, that's safe enough then," said Maligna. "They won't be able to take it unless you let them."

"Well," said Jadelli, "I suppose I could set them tasks, tell them they have to succeed in doing impossible things to win the Dragon Hoard."

"A splendid idea!" cried Maligna.

They went on talking for some time, and Maligna managed to persuade Jadelli that she was a powerful but kindly enchantress, who had only the kingdom's good at heart. This was by no means as unlikely as it sounds. Maligna could be very convincing when she tried.

Eventually, everything was decided, and, smiling a happy smile, Maligna got back into her golden chariot, and flew off.

Jadelli went to see her father, King Pumble, to warn him also, but she was almost too late.

The Quest had already arrived, and the fifty rowers were in the palace, being delightedly welcomed by the King.

"We have so few visitors," King Pumble was saying just as Jadelli came in.

"Well, your majesty," said Fearless, "as a matter of fact, we came to ask you if we could have our Dragon Hoard back. It did belong to us, once, long ago, before Stamp-Weed stole it."

Jadelli looked round at all the rowers. She was just deciding that Prince Fearless was handsome but a trifle pompous, when she caught sight of Jasleth, and an extraordinary thought popped into her head. She found herself thinking that he was just the sort of prince she would like to marry, although she had never thought of getting married before. And at the same moment that she was thinking this, Prince Jasleth was looking at her, and thinking how beautiful she was, but most of all, how she was just the sort of princess he would like to marry, although he had never thought of getting married before.

Just in time, Jadelli heard her father saying:

"The Dragon Hoard – oh, yes, I'm terrified of it. I never go near it if I can help –"

"But," Jadelli broke in quickly, "it's ours, and you

can't have it. Not unless you can do the magic tasks first." As she said it, she couldn't help thinking it a pity that now that nice prince with black hair and blue eyes would have to face all sorts of horrible dangers, or else go home disappointed.

"Jadelli!" cried the King.

"No, Father," said Jadelli firmly. "You know anyone who comes for the Dragon Hoard has to do the tasks."

"Do I?" asked King Pumble. He was rather a forgetful King, but, unlike most people, he knew he was, so he thought perhaps he might have forgotten this too.

"Yes, Father," said Jadelli in her firm voice.

"Oh – er – well, yes. I'm afraid," said the King apologetically to the rowers, "you'll have to, then."

"Of course, your majesty," said Fearless, grandly. "We're quite willing to behave in an honourable fashion."

"Oh – er – good – er –thank you," said Pumble, then whispered anxiously, "Jadelli, my dear, I can't seem to remember quite what the first task was."

"The first task," announced Jadelli, "is to tame my father's two fierce white horses. Nobody has ever been able to do it. They can run for three days without stopping, and they snort fire."

"Surely, my dear," muttered King Pumble, "you don't mean Pansy and Snowdrop?"

Jadelli put her finger to her lips and King Pumble, looking more anxious than ever, kept silent.

The fifty rowers were all talking among themselves, looking a bit pale and nervous. Eventually, Fearless said:

"We'll do it!"

"I must warn you," said Jadelli, sternly, "that many have perished in the attempt."

"We'll still do it," quavered Fearless.

"Then wait here," said Jadelli, "and I will tell the grooms to let them out in the big meadow, behind the palace."

The princess left the room and went down to the royal stables. There were Pansy and Snowdrop, the King's two white horses, both as gentle as lambs, tossing their long silky manes. They whinnied with pleasure when they saw Jadelli, and they wouldn't have dreamed of blowing out fire at her, even if they had been able to. But since the questors were insisting on attempting the task, Jadelli had to make sure that the two horses were fierce enough to frighten them away, or stop them. She took out some magic sugar, and gave a lump to Pansy and a lump to Snowdrop. Then she opened the stable door into the meadow, and quickly stood aside.

What a surprise it was to the two horses, suddenly to feel so fierce! They reared and stamped and neighed, and went galloping out into the meadow, throwing up their heels, and shouting to each other:

"Let's find somebody and eat them up!"

To their astonishment, long curls of blue smoke came from their nostrils, and little bright flames.

"Look at me!" yelled Snowdrop, prancing.

"Look at *me*!" yelled Pansy, trying to set an oak tree on fire.

Jadelli had meanwhile slipped out of the meadow and through a gate in the wall. She caught sight of

Jasleth and Onga and Fearless and one or two others, drawing straws to see who should go and try to tame the horses first. Even as she watched, Jasleth stood up and tightened his sword belt.

"Oh!" said Jadelli, and turned quite as pale as Jasleth had.

Jasleth went round the meadow on the outside, then got up on to the wall, and jumped down on the grass. Pansy and Snowdrop turned round, grinned at each other, and started pawing the ground.

"Nice horses," cooed Jasleth uncertainly. "Come to Uncle Jasleth then. On second thoughts – " he added, as Pansy and Snowdrop came racing towards him, blowing out fire, "On third thoughts – " said Jasleth, and ran for the wall. He just got up on it in time. Pansy and Snowdrop stood at the bottom, and showed their large teeth at him.

"Look here," said Jasleth from the wall, "you must find it awfully tiring, running about like that."

The horses laughed.

"Why not try to be tame, just to see how you like it," wheedled Jasleth. "I'll bet you've never had apples to eat, or sugar-lumps, or salt, or given people rides. You'd enjoy it, really you would. Now I'm just going to get down into the meadow, and then we'll all have a friendly little – Ow!" added Jasleth, as Pansy got the edge of his cloak in her teeth, and pulled him down flat on his face in the meadow.

"Look here," gasped Jasleth, picking himself up.

"Wait a minute!" yelled Jasleth, racing up the meadow, with Pansy and Snowdrop racing behind.

"Help!" howled Jasleth.

Just then he fell over a tree root.

Pansy and Snowdrop, snorting fire and smoke, were almost on top of him.

"I can't bear it!" cried Jadelli. She quickly took some magic dust from a little box in her girdle, and threw it into the meadow. In a second, Pansy and Snowdrop were bending over Jasleth, gently nosing at him, and asking him, in kind voices, if he was all right.

"You're tame!" croaked Jasleth. The two horses helped him up, and gave him a warm horse-kiss on each cheek. "I've done it!" shouted Jasleth. "I've succeeded at the task!"

All the rowers, who had been afraid to look, crowded excitedly into the meadow to tell Jasleth how brave and clever he was.

Jadelli, meanwhile, had gone back to the palace to think up another task, so off-putting as to make *The Quest* return home at once, without causing anyone any more trouble. Any other princess might have shed a tear or two perhaps at having to get a prince like Jasleth out of the way when she thought he was so nice, but Jadelli wasn't that sort of princess. She knew that tears wouldn't help either Jasleth or her kingdom, or even herself, so they remained unshed. Instead, she got out her spell-books, and magic potions, and pored over them until it was time for dinner.

Meantime, in the dusk, the questors had insisted on having a torchlight procession through the town, with Jasleth and Fearless proudly leading Pansy and Snowdrop. They made one of King Pumble's heralds walk in front, and shout out loudly how the brave rowers had tamed the King's terrible, fierce, fire-breathing horses. The herald kept raising his eyes to heaven, and muttering something Jasleth couldn't quite catch. As for King Pumble's subjects, they were turning to each other and saying:

"Who? *Pansy* and *Snowdrop*? What *are* they talking about? Has everyone gone mad?"

Pansy and Snowdrop just looked at their hoofs, and giggled.

All the rowers sat down in the hall with King Pumble and the princess, to have dinner. Prince Fearless sat next to King Pumble, and Jasleth found himself next to Jadelli. He told her all about his father's kingdom, omitting the distressing details about its present state, and she said she thought it sounded very nice. Jasleth said she must come and visit them.

When dinner was finished, Jadelli stood up and said:

"Now I have to tell you about the second task."

"My dear," said Pumble, "surely one is enough."

Jadelli took no notice.

"The second task," said Jadelli, not looking at Jasleth, "is to empty the pool in the palace garden into a single jug."

She had thought this sounded a nice impossible task, while not being a bit dangerous. When she had spoken, she smiled at Jasleth to say goodbye, and left the hall.

The rowers went down to the palace pool, and looked at it by starlight. It was a very big pool. On a small island in the middle, the black swans were lying in their nest.

"We'll never do it," said Jasleth.

"There might be a spell in one of Awful's books,"

said Fearless vaguely. "Or Onga could speak to his genie."

"I'm afraid I won't be able to," said Onga. He had got his headdress back from the sea-horse, but the salt water had taken the magic out of the feathers, so he couldn't use them.

"There must be an answer," said Jasleth. He walked all round the pool, and put in a stick to see how deep it was. It was rather deep.

"First of all," said Jasleth, "we'll have to get the water out, ready to go in the jug."

Everybody agreed that this was quite sensible.

"We could always have a chain of pails, fill them at the pool, and pass them along from hand to hand, like baling on the ship," said the twenty-eighth rower. "There are fifty of us after all. It shouldn't take *that* long."

"But the jug will overflow at the first pailful," said Fearless.

Everybody agreed that this was quite possible.

"Couldn't we ask the King," said Sillius, "if we could go on to the third task, and leave this one till last?"

"No," said Fearless.

"I think," said Jasleth, "we should go and ask the princess for help. She seems very nice, and she's much too beautiful to be unkind."

"All right," said Fearless. "I don't see why not, although I don't think she will agree. We'll toss up to see who'll go."

"I've got a gold coin," said Sillius. "No, I haven't," he added, looking puzzled and rummaging about in his pocket. "Well, I did have."

"Here you are," said Onga, picking up something from the grass. "You must have a hole in your pocket, and it fell through."

Jasleth gave a shout. Everybody jumped, and the swans woke up, and called out from their nest that some people were trying to get some sleep, *if* you don't mind.

"I've got it," whispered Jasleth.

"Got what?" asked Fearless, edging away, just in case.

"The answer," said Jasleth, "is a hole."

"A whole what?" asked Fearless.

"No, no," said Jasleth patiently. "You see, Sillius put a coin in his pocket, but there was hole, and the coin fell through. If he put another coin in, that would fall through, too. In fact," went on Jasleth, "however many coins he puts into his pocket while the hole is still there, they will fall out again."

"Well," said Fearless, coldly, "I'd realised that."

Sillius, who hadn't realised it, was groping around in the grass, looking for his coin again.

"You don't see what I mean, do you?" asked Jasleth.

"No," said Fearless with dignity.

"I do," said Onga, in his dark soft voice. "Jasleth means that if there's a hole in the bottom of the jug, each pailful of water we pour in will leak out again through the hole, and there'll be room for the next."

"Oh! I *see*!" shouted Fearless.

The swans came splashing over, and tried to bite him. The rowers apologised, and promised to be quieter.

"I shall never get the cygnets off to sleep again

now," complained the mother swan as she swam away.

When the swans were back in their nest, the thirty-sixth rower whispered:

"But no one must see the water running out of the jug, must they?"

"Well," said Jasleth, "if we can make our chain of fifty rowers stretch to that wall over there, just behind the poplars, we'll be all right. I'll show you."

He took them to the wall, and when they looked at it, what should they find but a fountain, no longer playing, and all choked up with weeds. From the fountain, an old water-drain ran down the wall, and at the bottom, opened into the sea.

"Put the jug over the mouth of the fountain, and the water will run down the drain," explained Jasleth, although he didn't really have to. The next thing was to see if they could reach. Instead of finding there weren't enough of them, they found there were too many. Jasleth told the rowers not to stand in a straight line, but to make the chain go round all the poplar trees. This worked, and now they were just right for the last rower to pour his bucket into a jug on the wall, although it did look rather peculiar.

Jasleth marked out the right line for the chain to follow with a piece of chalk, and the rowers went and got an earthenware jug from the palace kitchen. Onga knocked a big hole in the bottom. Then they went to bed, but as Prince Jasleth kept on thinking how marvellous Princess Jadelli was, he didn't get much sleep.

First thing in the morning they made one of the sleepy heralds wake everybody up, and tell them to

come out into the garden. Even King Pumble came, still in his nightcap which he had forgotten to take off, and without his crown which he had forgotten to put on. The princess came too, looking rather pale.

"I don't see how they can possibly do it," she said.

But they did.

Everyone gasped with admiration as bucket after bucket came out of the pool, up the slope, round one poplar tree, round another poplar tree, and another, and another, and another, then across the terrace into the jug. And the jug never overflowed.

"My word!" said King Pumble.

Eventually, Prince Fearless came up to them, and said:

"If your majesty and the princess would care to inspect the pool."

King Pumble and Jadelli went and looked in. Not a drop of water was left in it, only mud and reeds and some damp water-lilies.

"Well –" began King Pumble.

Just then the swans woke up, and there was a terrible scene, as they demanded to know why their pool had been emptied, and – "Hurry up and refill it, or we shall bite you!"

The pool was quickly refilled.

"Have we won the Dragon Hoard yet?" Jasleth asked Jadelli.

"No," said Jadelli hastily.

"I was rather afraid we hadn't," said Jasleth.

"I'll tell you the next task tonight," said Jadelli, and went to read through her spell-books again.

CHAPTER EIGHT

In which Jasleth asks for a golden orange

The moon was just looking through the palace window at the fifty rowers and King Pumble sitting down to dinner, when the princess came in.

"Here we go again," muttered the forty-second rower.

"The third task," said Princess Jadelli, "is to fetch a golden orange from the top of the mountain at the end of my father's kingdom."

This sounded suspiciously simple. They had all seen the mountain in the distance, a big rounded green thing not high enough even to have a snowcap, and they had heard, too, that there was a magic grove at the top where all the plums and apples and damsons and oranges were made of gold.

"However," went on Jadelli, "the orange must be given to my father before sunset tomorrow."

The rowers sighed in despair. The mountain was at least a day's journey away, and then they would have to climb it, which might take ages, and after that, they would be a day coming back, so it was quite hopeless.

"It's quite hopeless," said Jasleth.

Jadelli sat down and ate her dinner, and was delightful to everyone, especially Jasleth. She had already realised the trick the rowers had played with the jug and the water drain, but she thought they couldn't possibly get away with a trick this time. Even if they tried giving her father an ordinary golden orange, it would be no good, because the oranges from the magic grove all had a special perfume that could not be found anywhere else.

After dinner the rowers went into the garden to hold another meeting, although they were careful to go nowhere near the pool, as the swans were still very touchy.

"Even if we set out now," said Jasleth, "we couldn't get to the mountain and back by tomorrow's sunset."

"We can't go home without the Dragon Hoard," said Fearless. "Think what people would say."

Everybody sat on the grass and tried to think of a way of getting the orange, or a way of explaining to people at home why they had failed. At last Jasleth said:

"There *is* one chance."

"What's that?" asked Fearless, brightening up.

"You know I change into a raven every day, for an hour?" said Jasleth. "Well, I've found it's much quicker flying than walking. For one thing, there are no steep places to go round, or woods to get lost in, and you certainly never have to get out of the way for anyone else except the odd eagle in a bad mood and that doesn't happen often. I was thinking, if I set off now, and start towards the mountain, whenever I change into a raven I shall be able to go much faster than any of you, even if it is only for an hour. Of course," he added, "it might not work, but it's worth a try, and we don't stand a chance of getting the orange otherwise."

Everyone cheered him, although very softly, in case the swans heard, and ten minutes later Jasleth was walking across the fields behind the palace, towards the round green mountain.

By the time dawn was in the sky, Jasleth was beginning to think it wasn't such a good idea after all. He watched the stars going out, and the sun coming up, and tried to pretend his feet weren't getting sore, and not to count his yawns. He got hungry, too, but luckily a farmer went by in a cart, and gave him a ride for a mile or so, and a tomato sandwich to eat. After he left the farmer, Jasleth walked on, and whistled to show himself how cheerful he really was. It got very hot and dusty, and he would like to have stopped and asked for a drink of water, but he thought he'd better not, as it would take time. On the horizon, the round mountain did seem a bit nearer. Jasleth thought he could just make out the dim outline of woods, and the dark places where there were caves.

He didn't change into a raven until quite late, but when it happened it was a nice change from walking. Up and up went Jasleth, flying as fast as he could, and soon he was getting near to the mountain, so near that he really could see the woods on its sides. As he came nearer still, he could make out the glitter where little streams bubbled along. Because he was flying and not walking on the ground, he was already half-way up. He flapped his tired wings even harder, and was nearly at the top, when – whoosh – ! He'd changed again. This time he fell into a mountain pool.

When he climbed out, a couple of wood nymphs were sitting on the bank in fits of giggles.

"Excuse me," said Jasleth, shaking off some of the water, "but am I going the right way to get to the magic grove with golden oranges?"

The nymphs just went on screaming with laughter. Jasleth felt like giving them both a good push, and seeing how they liked falling head first into a cold pool, but decided that wouldn't be a very gallant or princely action. When he saw he wasn't going to get an answer, he walked on into the trees, and fairly quickly he came out on a bare slope, where the sun beat down and soon dried him out.

There was still a long way to go. The sun got lower as Jasleth got higher, and he began to think it wasn't much use as he'd never be able to get to King Pumble's palace by sunset. Still, he went on, because it seemed silly to turn back after he'd already got so far.

Near the top of the mountain, Jasleth found an avenue of trees. There was a little path, and the sides of it were bordered with the most beautiful flowers. As he went further, Jasleth saw that every third paving stone was made of pearl, and every fourth of silver, and every fifth of gold.

"Well, at least this must be the right way," thought Jasleth.

Just then a squirrel came rushing across the path, and it had bright golden fur. It was gone again, up a tree, in a moment, but, as it went up, Jasleth saw that it was carrying a golden nut in its golden paws.

And then, suddenly, he was in the magic grove.

It was filled with the most wonderful scent from

all the trees growing there. Their trunks were like emeralds, and their leaves were like rubies, and from their silver boughs hung clusters of glowing, gleaming, golden fruit: pears and peaches, cherries and damsons, apricots and apples. And on the biggest tree of all, right in the middle of the grove, were the largest, most beautifully perfumed, golden oranges.

Jasleth would have liked to look round at everything, but he knew there wasn't time, so he strode forward and put up his hand to pick the orange hanging lowest down. But before he could, something came whisking out of the tree and slapped his hand hard.

"Naughty!" said a sharp voice. "*Bad!* Mustn't!"

Jasleth looked up into the ruby leaves, but he couldn't see anyone. He looked over his shoulder, too, and even behind the tree, but there was nobody there.

'I must have imagined it,' thought Jasleth, although he knew he hadn't because his hand still hurt. Nevertheless he reached up a second time, and –

SWISH – SLAP!

It happened again.

"Naughty!" repeated the voice. "Naughty, bad, *mustn't!*"

Jasleth backed away, and stared up at the tree, rubbing his hand. After a moment he thought that perhaps someone was playing a joke on him, so he said in a loud voice:

"*Why* mustn't I?"

To his surprise, the voice immediately answered:

"Because I say so."

"Well," said Jasleth, "I don't think that's much of

a reason. I don't even know who you are. You might just as well say to me 'Throw yourself off the mountain' and I'd say 'Why?', and you'd say 'Because I say so', and then I suppose you'd expect me to do it."

"Not at all," said the voice. "And I wouldn't dream of saying such a thing. All I say is, you *mustn't* pick any of the golden oranges."

"Well, who are you?" asked Jasleth, who wasn't very keen on talking to people he couldn't see.

"I am the Guardian of the Orange Tree," said the voice. And then out stepped a most beautiful bird. It wasn't surprising Jasleth hadn't seen it to begin with, as it was all ruby-coloured, like the leaves, with a tall golden crest and emerald feet. It was its long silver tail, Jasleth now saw, that it had used to slap him with.

"Well," said Jasleth, "it really is rather important. I wonder," he added to himself, "if a golden plum would do for King Pumble instead."

"I might as well tell you," said the bird, who had overheard, "that all the trees in the magic grove have guardians. The guardian bird of the plum tree has an even longer tail than I have."

Jasleth looked about him worriedly. Already the glow in the sky was deepening, and in another hour the sun would have set. Jasleth thought the guardian bird, for all its sharp voice and slappy tail, had rather an understanding sort of face, so he went up to it, and told it about the quest for the Dragon Hoard, and the tasks, and how important it all was.

The bird nodded wisely, and gave itself a little preen.

"Of course, you do realise," it said eventually,

"that you won't get back to King Pumble's palace on time."

"It doesn't seem very likely, I admit," agreed Jasleth, "but I think I ought to try."

"I'll tell you what," said the bird. "The magic law says no human being must take fruit from the grove, but the guardian bird is allowed to if it wants. You seem a nice, honest sort of prince. I'll take your golden orange down to King Pumble's palace, and show it to him. That should be good enough, shouldn't it?"

"Oh, yes," said Jasleth. "I'm sure it would be all right. But how will you get down there in time?"

"Oh, we guardian birds, you know," said the bird, offhandedly, "we can fly faster than a flash of lightning. It won't take me more than a minute or so to reach the palace. However," it added, looking down at Jasleth intently, out of its big green eyes, "if I go away from the mountain, you'll have to stay here and guard the orange tree in my place."

"But of course," cried Jasleth delightedly. "Anyway, if you fly as fast as all that, you won't be gone five minutes, will you?"

"Well," said the bird, "I was thinking. I never see anything of the world, shut up here in my tree all day and all night, year in and year out. I was wondering if you would stay here all night, and then I could have a look round the kingdom, and enjoy myself."

"Oh – er – yes," said Jasleth. He felt he couldn't refuse after the bird had been so kind to him, but he wasn't sure he liked the idea of spending all night in a cold magic tree. Besides, if someone had to guard the place all the time, what were they guarding it from?

"Oh, just the odd dragon, you know," said the bird unworriedly. "Or the odd enchanter; nothing much. And nobody may come along at all. Anyway, it's very kind of you. I'll be off now, before the sun sets. See you in the morning."

So saying, the bird plucked a golden orange with its beak, and flew up out of the grove, and was gone in a flash. Jasleth saw it had dropped a few ruby feathers on the grass, and bent down to pick them up. Then he climbed into the tree, and hid himself in the thick leaves, and hoped it would soon be morning.

Had Jasleth been able to see Maligna as clearly as she was able to see him, he would have been down off that tree, and down off that mountain, quicker than any guardian bird.

Needless to say, she had been glued to her magic looking-glass ever since she had been to see Jadelli, and she wasn't a bit pleased at the way things were going. Jasleth and the other rowers all seemed to be having their usual run of improbable good luck, and she was alarmed at the glances she had intercepted between Jadelli and Jasleth. Now, however, she thought she had the ideal opportunity to put a spoke in Jasleth's wheel for good and all. So, while Jasleth was sitting huddled up in the magic orange tree, thinking about Princess Jadelli, and how he was going to save his father from ruin any day now, Maligna was appearing in the houses of her nastiest friends, and telling them if they had ever wanted to steal a golden orange from the magic grove on King Pumble's mountain, now was their chance.

"That bossy bird's gone away for the night,"

Maligna told them all, "and there's only some silly human being up in the tree, shivering with fright."

Poor Jasleth!

To start with, things hadn't gone badly. First of all, there was a lot of rustling, and something tugged at the branches. Jasleth thought it was a dragon, and didn't know what to do. He was trying to draw his sword without falling out of the tree, when he saw it was only a small golden monkey. The golden animals, and the monkey of course, were allowed to take what fruit they liked, so Jasleth sat back, and let it pick an orange.

A bit later, he felt the tugging again, and thought the monkey had come back, or it was a squirrel or something. However this time it really was a dragon, only a very small one. Jasleth was so scared that he could only think of one thing to do, so he leaned down and hit the dragon sharply on the nose with the ruby feathers the bird had dropped, and yelled out:

"Naughty! Bad! Mustn't!"

The dragon screamed and ran away. This heartened Jasleth quite a bit. He was still sitting there, planning the best way to tell Princess Jadelli how he had frightened off an enormous dreadful dragon, while sounding modest at the same time, when there was an awful din just outside the grove, and the next minute three horrible enchanters came barging up to the orange tree, and began shaking it with all their strength.

"Here, hang on!" cried Jasleth, hanging on himself.

"What's that?" said the nastiest-looking enchanter.

"Oh, it's only the human being," said the second nastiest. "Let's change him into a stone or some-

131

thing." Jasleth promptly decided that this one was the nastiest enchanter after all.

"Naughty! Bad!" tried Jasleth, while his teeth rattled.

Just then a couple of bad-tempered ghosts came howling up the hill, tripping over their long robes and their chains, and after these, a witch on a broomstick, whose hat blew off in the face of the monster who was coming up behind. After the monster, came two or three dragons – big ones this time – an enchantress in a chariot drawn by three-headed lions all squabbling and growling at each other and even at the other heads on their own bodies, followed by a simply enormous giant with a big cudgel.

Jasleth could hardly hear his teeth chattering over all the noise

Everything thundered to a halt round the orange tree.

The first enchanter looked angrily at the other two.

"Who invited all these people?" he snapped. "Was it you?"

"Not me," said the other two enchanters as one.

"And it certainly wasn't me," added Jasleth, but nobody took any notice of him.

"All these people," the first enchanter was saying bad-temperedly. "If they all take golden oranges, there won't be enough to go round. Go away!" he added to the monster. "Shoo!" he added to the ghosts. "*We* were here *first*, your honour," he added to the giant. "Would you ask your nice pussy," he added to the enchantress, "to get off my foot?"

A frightful argument quickly broke out. The enchantress said she wanted three oranges, the witch

wanted four, and the monster insisted it needed five, one for each of its heads. As for the ghosts, they began to run round the tree, hitting it with their chains in the hope that an orange might fall down. The lions, meanwhile, were trying to bite everyone and the enchanters were conjuring up howling gales and thunderbolts and lightning flashes, and throwing them in all directions.

Maligna had made the mistake of telling too many people about the oranges. Everybody was much too busy being greedy to bother to change Jasleth into a stone or something worse, although they would probably have got round to it eventually. The first enchanter was just trying to change the enchantress into a hippopotamus, and the enchantress was getting her own back by making it rain treacle over him; the ghosts were fighting with the lions; the monster was digging up the tree roots while the witch hit him on the head with her broomstick; the giant was heaving at the top of the tree to pull it up, and a most ghastly storm was banging and booming all around them, when Jasleth was almost knocked over backwards, and who should be sitting on the branch next to him, but – the guardian bird!

"Well," remarked the bird, "you don't seem to be much good at guarding trees, do you?"

Jasleth tried to explain, or, at any rate, to make excuses, but the bird couldn't hear him above the noise. Instead of trying to, it shook out its wing feathers, and bawled in a most terrible voice:

"Naughty! *Bad!* MUSTN'T!!"

There was silence at once. Even the storm stopped, and there were only a few last timid flashes of lightning that quickly died away. It seemed the bird must have some special magic power, so it had been a bit unfair of it to expect Jasleth to manage in its place.

"Now," said the bird to all the enchanters and ghosts and everybody else, "you ought to be ashamed. Go away at once. You know the rules here."

The enchanters shook their fists, and the ghosts shook their chains, and the lions growled, but everyone stopped trying to get at the golden oranges. The monster just turned and went off down the hill. Fairly soon all the others did the same. Even the witch flew off on her broomstick, although she managed to whack the giant on the nose as she went past.

"Thank goodness you came back," said Jasleth to the bird.

"I quite agree," said the bird.

"Why *did* you come back?" asked Jasleth, hoping to take the bird's mind off what had just happened. He thought the bird might do something dreadful to him for not looking after the tree properly.

"I came back," said the bird, "because when I got out into the world, I found it full of nasty people like those enchanters and that witch. I thought to myself 'I'm much better off in my nice quiet comfortable tree.' And what did I find when I got back here?"

"I'm very sorry," said Jasleth.

"It's not your fault," said the bird, patting his shoulder kindly with its wing. "It's taught me a lesson. It's my job to guard this tree, and it's no good leaving your jobs for other people to do. Something will always go wrong."

"Well," said Jasleth, "I suppose I'd better be getting back."

"Of course you must," said the bird. "I showed King Pumble and the princess the golden orange, by the way, so your third task is completed."

It waved Jasleth off, and Jasleth walked down the mountain and back to King Pumble's palace. It took ages, even with an hour's flying time thrown in.

All the questors cheered him as he staggered through the gate in the middle of the next afternoon, and begged to be told what had happened. However, Jasleth went straight to bed because he was so tired. He didn't tell the story of his adventure until the next morning at breakfast.

Everybody was thrilled and horrified at the happenings in the tree, and they sounded truly dreadful when he told them. So dreadful in fact that Jasleth even frightened himself all over again, and had to sit down. As for the princess, she knew now that she wouldn't dare set the questors any other tasks, because Jasleth always seemed to be the one who did them, and they always seemed so dangerous.

She went up to her room, however, and had a look through her books, and wondered what were the best spells to stop measles and whooping cough and drought and flood, just in case.

CHAPTER NINE

In which the Dragon Hoard is finally won – Hurrah!

She really didn't know what to do. She wanted Jasleth to be happy, which meant giving the rowers the Dragon Hoard, and she wanted her father's subjects to be happy, which meant *not* giving the rowers the Dragon Hoard. Eventually she decided to tell them that though there were no more tasks, to get the Hoard, they would still have to fight the dreadful dragon that guarded it. She hoped that the sound of the dragon would be enough to put anybody off.

So she asked one of the heralds to tell everyone to come to a meeting in the palace hall at dusk, and, to give herself encouragement, she went and put on the biggest pearl headdress she could find.

"Here comes the princess," muttered the eighteenth rower. "I wonder what it will be *this* time. Making the sun stand still, I shouldn't be surprised."

"Somebody go and say that the princess is about to announce what the fourth task is," said King Pumble, who was, by now, getting the hang of things.

"There isn't a fourth task," said Jadelli. She turned to the questors. "All you have to do now," she told them, "is to slay the fierce dragon that guards the Hoard."

There was a sort of half-hearted cheer. Nobody was too keen on the idea of dragon-slaying.

"But before you set out," went on Jadelli, "I suggest you all read this book about the dragon. It tells you exactly what it's like."

And she handed to Prince Fearless a simply enormous black book, bound in gold, entitled: *THE HOARD DRAGON. NOT TO BE READ BY THE FAINT-HEARTED.*

Prince Fearless opened it at the first page. He took one look at the dragon's picture, and dropped the book on Jasleth's toe.

"It's rather big," said Jasleth.

"It says as long as a hundred men, all stretched out, holding each other's heels!" trembled Fearless.

"I meant the book," said Jasleth.

"I meant the dragon," said Fearless. "It's as high as a house, with scales no sword can pierce, and four pairs of eyes, each looking a different way."

"Oh yes," said Jasleth.

"And it's black, and it breathes fire. Its mouth is so huge it can swallow an army at one gulp. It once did."

"Did it?" asked Jasleth.

"It has nine hundred and fifty-four teeth," said Fearless, "each three inches long and as sharp as a needle."

"A needle?" repeated Jasleth.

"It never sleeps," said Fearless, "and it hasn't been fed for a hundred years. Its last meal was the army I mentioned earlier."

"Let's go home," said Jasleth.

"And when it roars, it sounds like fifty thunderstorms all going at once," said Fearless.

"I mean," said Jasleth, "think how everyone at home must miss us."

"When it shakes itself, the earth trembles," said Fearless.

"Only too glad to have us back," went on Jasleth.

"And when it breathes fire out, all the trees in the grove smoulder."

". . . with or without the Dragon Hoard," finished Jasleth.

"We can't," said Fearless.

"No, we can't," said Jasleth.

"I meant we can't go home without the Dragon Hoard," said Fearless.

"I meant we can't fight the dragon," said Jasleth

The questors decided to go into the garden and hold a meeting of their own.

Princess Jadelli followed them out, and hid behind a poplar tree, to see what they would decide to do. She hadn't had any trouble in finding them as Sillius had nearly fallen into the pool and the swans had all started shouting at him.

It was dark among the trees, although starlight was striping the garden like a zebra. You could hear all the fountains tinkling to themselves, and the mother birds telling their children to be quiet and go to bed. Sometimes the flowers would mutter in their sleep.

Fearless had brought out a small lantern, and by the light of it the rowers were looking through the dragon book, and frightening themselves silly.

"It's not even as if it's a nice normal sort of dragon," complained the twenty-third rower.

"It's not normal at all," added the twenty-ninth.

"Not a bit normal," agreed the thirtieth.

"The thing is," said Fearless, "we can't go home without the Dragon Hoard. We should be laughed at. Our parents would be ashamed of us."

Jasleth thought he heard someone sigh a deep sad sigh behind one of the trees, but it must have been the breeze.

"So," said Fearless, "I suggest we do what we did before, that is, we'll draw straws. After all, if the dragon can swallow an army at one gulp, it'll make short work of us if we all go together."

"Just a snack," agreed Jasleth.

"So," went on Fearless, "there's no point in all of us getting eaten. In fact, if only one of us goes, the dragon may not even see him. And if he succeeds — think of the glory and the honour! His name will go down in legend for ever and ever."

So they put the straws in a clay jar, and mixed them around, and then drew one each.

"Oh," said Jasleth.

"Well, well," said Fearless, "it seems to be you, Jasleth. Congratulations."

"Wait a minute," said Onga's deep dark voice. "Jasleth got the shortest straw last time. It isn't fair for him to do all the dangerous work again. I'll do it, Jasleth."

"Or I will," added the forty-seven other questors in rather guilty unison.

"I," said Fearless, "as leader of the expedition, will do it."

But Jasleth slowly shook his head. "No," he said, looking very brave and handsome in the starlight. "I drew the straw. It's my duty to go and fight the

140

dragon. Only," he added, "do you think I could have a glass of water first? I feel rather odd."

Jadelli, meanwhile, was hurrying back to the palace to get a few magic potions that she could throw over the dragon to stop it eating Jasleth.

It was some distance to the magic oak grove.

The path ran among wild thick woodland, so dark that the moon hardly ever shone through. Jasleth and Onga and Fearless kept stumbling over tree-roots, and banging into each other and thinking they were the dragon, and yelling and drawing their swords. Jadelli, who was gliding behind, made no noise at all. She was wearing a pair of her witch-school shoes, that carried her along an inch or so above the ground. In her hand she had a bag of powders and potions, and in her heart she was hoping that the dragon would be looking the other way with its four eyes when Jasleth arrived, and that he would be so alarmed at it that he would go home immediately, without stopping to fight.

Once they came to a huge old tree-trunk, lying in a clearing, and the moon chose that moment to shine in through the leaves.

"It's the dragon," croaked Fearless, but when they realised it was only a tree-trunk, he patted Jasleth's shoulder kindly and said, "Chin up, dear fellow. Nothing to be scared of, you know."

Jasleth was doing his very best to be brave and behave the way a prince should. He was remembering the time at the start of his adventures when he had gone round looking – actually *looking* – for five-headed monsters to fight! It was what every prince hoped for, wasn't it? To slay a dragon and find his fortune and marry a beautiful princess, too, if there happened to be one around.

"The thing is," Jasleth thought, "until you actually have a hundred-man-long dragon to slay, you don't realise how dangerous it can be."

The Dragon Book had told them that a few yards away from the grove, there was a big black stone, and suddenly Fearless fell right over it.

"Almost there!" he quavered.

"It's all right," said Jasleth. "I'll go on alone from here."

"Well if you insist," gasped Fearless.

"Call us if you need us," added Onga.

"Thank you," said Jasleth. "Perhaps – perhaps, if I don't – don't come back, you'd give my love to my father and mother and sister, and – er – Princess Jadelli, too, if you wouldn't mind."

"Anything!" cried Fearless.

"Of course you'll come back," encouraged Onga.

"Well, just in case – " and so saying, Jasleth turned away, and walked on into the wood.

Jadelli had to slip round one or two tree-trunks to avoid being seen by Onga and Fearless, and it took her a minute to catch up with Jasleth again. By that time he had just reached the edge of the magic grove.

The trees were very tall, but the middle of the grove was an open space with a single oak growing in it. The moon was pouring in silver glow, and, up in the tree, something caught the light, and glittered and glittered. It was a great casket, all gold, with long curved handles, just like the painting on the sail of

The Quest. It was the Dragon Hoard! For a moment Jasleth was so excited he forgot to be afraid.

Then he remembered, and looked round for the dragon.

The book had said the dragon would be curled round and round the trunk, its eyes looking in all directions at once, and long smoke rings coming out of its nostrils. Its scales would gleam like black oil.

Jasleth looked at the tree, first in fright, then in surprise. After this, he looked round the grove. Then he went cautiously into the grove, then less cautiously, and finally he strode from end to end, peering under bushes, and round the branches of the oak trees. There was no dragon, anywhere.

It was about five minutes later that he found the small, neatly-printed notice tied on to a branch near the foot of the Dragon Hoard tree.

At the top was that day's date, and underneath it said:

HAVE GONE TO THE DENTIST. BACK TO-MORROW AFTERNOON.

It so happened that the dragon was very concerned about its nine hundred and fifty-four teeth. Not that there was ever anything wrong with them, but it always tried to have a check-up once a year, and to have them scaled. Because it had so many teeth, the scaling took rather a long time: a whole day and a night and a morning, in fact. Its dentist used to get very tired.

Jasleth was so glad and astonished that the first thing he did was to lean against a tree, and go off into helpless laughter.

Fearless and Onga, who heard him laughing,

looked at each other and wondered if they should run away or go and see what had happened, instead.

Fairly soon, however, they heard Jasleth's voice calling them. He didn't sound as if he were in any danger, or needed any help, he just sounded very pleased about something or other. So, with drawn swords, just in case, Onga and Fearless went through the trees and into the grove, and saw what Jasleth had found. Quite quickly they were all laughing and congratulating each other, and planning the best way to climb up and get the Dragon Hoard down.

Just then there was a soft rustle as the leaves parted, and the three princes looked thoroughly alarmed. But it was only the Princess Jadelli, and not the dragon coming back early.

"I'm so glad you didn't have to fight the dragon after all," said Jadelli. "And now you've won the Dragon Hoard."

"Yes," said Fearless. "It's ours. We've completed all the tasks."

"I know you have," said Jadelli. "And I've a confession to make. I made up all those tasks myself. You see, I had to. I had to try to stop your taking the Dragon Hoard any way that I could, because, when you take it, my father's kingdom will have dreadful bad luck, drought and floods and measles and whooping cough."

"How do you know that?" asked Fearless.

"A powerful enchantress," said Jadelli, "came all the way to see me from a far country, to warn me about it. She'd seen it in a magic glass that foretold the future. Once the Dragon Hoard is taken, she said, the most awful things will happen to us. So, dear

Prince Fearless and dear Prince Onga and dearest Prince Jasleth, all I can do is to beg you, although you have won it, to leave the Hoard where it is."

It really was very difficult to be hard-hearted with beautiful Princess Jadelli gazing at them so sadly with her large intelligent jade-green eyes.

"I don't know what to say," said Fearless. "We shall look so silly going back without it. On the other hand, we can't possibly bring you all this bad luck."

"Without a doubt," said Onga, "you must keep the Dragon Hoard."

Jasleth, meanwhile, had been leaning against an oak tree thinking. Whenever anyone spoke about powerful enchantresses, he always thought of Maligna, and now he had the funniest sort of feeling -- the oddest sort of feeling --

"Princess Jadelli," said Jasleth, "what was this enchantress's name?"

"She didn't tell me," said Jadelli. "But she wore wonderful clothes and a long golden veil. I did notice that she had one or two bats in her hair, but then enchantresses often do strange --"

"It's Maligna!" cried Jasleth.

"Bless you!" said Fearless, who was only half listening, and thought somebody had sneezed.

"Who?" asked Onga.

"Don't you remember?" said Jasleth. "The wicked enchantress who made my sister so good it was silly, and made me change into a raven for an hour every day for a year?"

"Ah, yes," said Onga.

"Oh, her," said Fearless.

"Well, Maligna," said Jasleth, "had bats in her

hair. She didn't come in a winged-serpent chariot by any chance, did she?" Jasleth asked Jadelli.

"Yes," said Jadelli. "She did."

"Well, you know what *I* think," said Jasleth, and he told her what he thought.

He got it almost all right, about the storms, and the mud rain, and the log and its bad advice, and the mermaids, and the hullabaloo in the magic grove. Anyhow nobody doubted Jasleth for a moment, and Jadelli said if ever she saw Maligna again, she would teach her a lesson. Everybody laughed, because no one believed that so beautiful a princess could bear a grudge. However, when an enchantress says something like that, especially if she is young and beautiful, and fresh from witch-school, you can be sure she means it.

It was Onga who climbed up into the tree and took the Dragon Hoard. He dropped it down, and Jasleth and Fearless caught it in their cloaks. It wasn't very heavy, and it had a big lid with an enormous clasp. At first they thought perhaps they ought to wait and take it back to the other questors before they opened it, but they were so excited they couldn't wait.

It was rather like having a birthday and Christmas and Easter and New Year present all rolled up into one.

Fearless opened the casket. Inside, a big red cloth had been laid over the contents, and on top of the cloth was a scroll with something written on it in gold lettering.

"What does it say?" asked Jasleth and Onga.

"It says," said Fearless, "that this box contains a collection of ancient and wonderful stones. The green

stones are Luck Stones, one of which will bring constant good luck to the wearer. The red stones are Feast Stones. Set on any bare table, they will produce a splendid feast, big enough to feed a hundred persons. The yellow stones are Gold Stones. All metal they touch will be changed at once into gold."

Everyone stood staring at the red cloth. At last Jasleth went forward and drew it off, and a wonderful, sparkling light burst up from the jewels lying there, scarlet, and melon-yellow and young-leaf-green.

"Plenty for everybody, fortunately," remarked Onga wisely.

He even climbed back up the tree, and left a

handful glittering on the branch where the casket had been, so that the dragon wouldn't be too upset when it came back.

Actually, the dragon never even noticed. It hadn't bothered to look up at the branch where the Hoard was for hundreds of years.

King Pumble gave an especially nice feast to celebrate. It went on all night. Prince Fearless presented King Pumble with several stones, and made a grand and romantic speech, and then turned to Jasleth and said:

"And, of all of us, none has been so brave and noble as Prince Jasleth."

Everybody cheered loudly.

"So," added Fearless apologetically, "I'm afraid, Jasleth, you've won the hand of my sister, Princess Poppy-Lily."

Jasleth looked alarmed. Fearless went rather red. There was a dreadful silence which went on and on, and was suddenly broken by the sound of somebody sobbing. Everyone looked round to see who it was, and there was Prince Sillius, weeping into the apple-pie and cream.

Fearless asked him what the matter was, and Sillius told him between sobs that he had fallen madly in love with Princess Poppy-Lily the moment he saw her, and wasn't there some brave deed he could go out and do now, to see if he could do better than Jasleth?

"There, there," said Jasleth kindly. "If it's as bad as all that, you must marry her, and not me."

"Of course," added Onga, and winked.

Fearless just looked relieved.

Sillius soon cheered up, and had another helping of apple-pie, and said he couldn't understand why it tasted so salty all of a sudden.

"Actually," said Jasleth to Jadelli, "I was rather hoping I could ask *you* to marry me."

"I was rather hoping so, too," said Jadelli.

"What a good idea," said King Pumble, who had overheard. "Haven't had a good wedding round here for years."

There was great rejoicing. Everyone rejoiced, even the black swans, who sent Fearless a very nice note saying they were sorry for biting him. King Pumble had a wonderful time now he had eventually found out what the Dragon Hoard was. He went gaily round the palace and the town, humming little tunes to himself and producing enormous feasts that nobody could ever eat because there was too much, and changing all the metal he could find into gold. Soon the cooks were cooking in golden saucepans that melted, the gardeners were pruning the poplars with golden shears that didn't cut very well, and all the door-plates in the town were gold and there were even golden bells round the necks of the cows.

The wedding of Jasleth and Jadelli was a splendid affair.

Sillius said he had never eaten so much, or felt so lucky, or fallen over, under, or into so many golden chairlegs, tables or soup tureens in his life.

There was, however, one person who was not a bit pleased. That was Maligna.

She watched all the festivities with absolute fury, with all her bats up in curlers and hairpins, and Sweetie and Poppet tied up to a tree. She still hadn't sorted her spells out, but she was so angry she felt she simply had to do something. She snatched up a big black jar labelled LIGHTNING and threw all the contents into her cauldron. She wanted the lightning to strike King Pumble's palace, and bring it crashing down all over the rowers and Jadelli and the King and especially Jasleth. However, the toad had mixed something else in with the lightning, and it didn't strike King Pumble's palace; it struck Maligna's instead.

There was an awful booming, rolling, thundering crash, and Maligna found herself flying downwards at a terrific rate with all her crooked towers and turrets flying after her.

She ended up in the cellar with all her spell-books and her cauldron, which fell over her head, while her palace settled over the cellar roof and the door.

She found she couldn't get out.

Only a spell could help her, she decided, but all her really important spells were in a toad-muddle, so she had to go right back to the beginning of the book and start all over again, with the most simple magic she had learned at witch-school.

"I'll darn that toad up in a sock!" she raged. "I'll change that Jasleth into a toasting fork! I'll change – I'll – !"

It took her ages to get out, and she couldn't even make herself a cup of stinging-nettle tea, or a throttle-weed sandwich, to cheer herself up.

PART FOUR
Final Magic

CHAPTER TEN

In which Jasleth comes home, and Maligna gets a present

It was quite a long time before *The Quest* set sail for home.

It was on a clear day, with a strong breeze blowing in the right direction, that the rowers said goodbye to King Pumble and the swans, with whom they were on the best of terms by now, and took their treasure, and went down the beach to the ship.

Jadelli kissed her father, and said she would see him soon and not to worry and to remember to put on his fur muffler when the weather turned chilly. Then she got into the ship, next to Jasleth, the rowers pulled on their oars, and the ship slid out into the blue sea.

It made a nice change for them to have an enchantress on their side. Jadelli made sure with her spells that they had simply beautiful weather all the way back to King Purple's kingdom. Every night, before they went to bed, she gave the forty-nine rowers and Jasleth magic lessons.

The dolphins and porpoises and mermaids would come and sit around in the evening water to watch. As the last colours faded out of the sky, you could hear them chanting after Jadelli:

"Throw in half a pinch of bee's fur, and stir vigorously."

There were all sorts of explosions under the sea after that, as the mermaids tried out the spells and did them wrong.

"I think all this is most distressing," said an elderly whale. "Can the young find nothing more useful to do?"

When *The Quest* sailed over the kingdom of Queen Emeraldis, all the fish went and hid, and the mermaids dived into the seaweed forests. Only Queen Emeraldis came bravely up to the surface, and, her face as pink as her shell chariot, said:

"We would like you to know how very sorry we are about the – er – unfortunate incident that happened last time you were here."

"Oh no, really," said Fearless gallantly. "We enjoyed it."

"Please accept this casket of rare corals," said Queen Emeraldis, holding out a beautiful box to them, "as a token of our repentance."

Everyone said "Thank you", and "Awfully nice of you", and "Really, we didn't mind a bit", and Emeraldis felt much better by the time she drove back down to her kingdom.

When they came to Awful's island, they found that the whole beach had been laid out with coloured stones, and the demons and monsters were playing skittles to their hearts' content. The alligator and the crocodiles had found a nice lagoon to snooze in, and had hung up the washing to dry on their harps. They were using the drum as a tea table. The snakes were lying about in deck chairs, eating jelly and getting fat

in case Awful came back and tried to make them wear their uniforms again.

They begged the rowers to stop, but the rowers thought it all looked a bit rough and noisy, and just then the nanny-goat pulled open one of the red glass palace windows, and emptied a soup tureen over everyone underneath.

"Think we'd better not put in," said Fearless. "Bit pressed for time, you know, just at the moment."

The nanny-goat was heaving an enormous jam roll out of the window as they rowed away.

Of course, they did stay a few days at the stone island, where the genie was having a wonderful time. The king had built him a special palace, with a silver roof and copper pillars, and the ceilings in each room were twelve feet high, so the genie wouldn't bang his head. When Onga told him that the sea water had taken the magic out of his headdress, the genie put it back at once with a flip of his fingers, but there was such an awful crash of thunder as the genie did it, that the rowers rather wished that Onga hadn't asked.

The genie shook hands with everybody before they left, except Sillius, who had remembered some urgent business elsewhere.

The Quest eventually reached King Purple's kingdom on a hot sunny day. The sky was bright blue, and there was only one small cloud to be seen, slowly drifting and changing its shape overhead. The palace gleamed on its little rise, and, sure enough, there on the roof was King Purple, Fearless' father, chatting to the eagles, just the same as when they left.

All the people came rushing down to the quay, throwing flowers and waving. The Princess Poppy-Lily leaned out of her window and waved too, and her peacocks tried to climb up on each others' shoulders to see. The royal trumpeters picked up their trumpets, and ran out and blew a fanfare, and the drummers ran out and drummed, all out of time with each other, because they were so excited.

"Whatever is all this noise?" wondered King Purple. "Oh, good," he said to the eagles. "It's Fearless back again. We must put up a flag or something!"

Rather slowly and unsteadily, because he was a stout sort of king, and his robe and the eagles would keep getting in the way, King Purple climbed up the flagstaff, and raised the royal flag in Fearless' honour.

"Better have a special feast, too," he muttered, trying to climb down again. "Fearless'll be upset if I don't."

Just then his foot slipped, and King Purple slid all the way down the flagstaff, and fell off on top of his secretary, who had just arrived underneath.

When they had sorted themselves out, and the secretary had stopped saying "Oomph!" and "Ooch!", who should come bounding up the stairs but Prince Fearless.

"Father, I've brought back the Dragon Hoard!" cried Fearless.

"Well done," said King Purple. "I've put a flag up, and we'll have a feast."

"But Father, don't you want to *see* the Dragon Hoard?"

"Oh no, my boy. Just put it up in the attic with all the rest of the junk. Now, turkey or chicken for dinner?"

Fearless said he didn't care, and went away and sulked.

However, the feast was a great success. All the rowers cheered each other and themselves, and Prince Sillius asked if he could marry Princess Poppy-Lily. Poppy-Lily giggled, and her peacocks told him that he would have to behave himself, and treat them in the manner to which they were accustomed.

In the morning, the various rowers said they must be going, and began to take ships for their respective lands, carrying their share of the treasure and the Hoard with them. Fearless asked Onga to stay, but Onga said there was a princess he really must go home and marry. He took one of his magic feathers, made a small fire, and threw in some special powder. Then he drew a ring in the ashes round the fire with the feather, and what should appear in the ring but a magic picture of Onga's princess. She had long hair like ebony silk, and a dark silky skin, and her eyes were like the eyes of a deer. She was lovely. Jasleth and Fearless agreed that Onga should go home and marry her at once. Just then the princess caught sight of them.

"Hallo, Onga!" she cried, and waved, and all the bracelets on her arm clanked together. She had a pet cheetah that kept peering out of the magic ring at them, and trying to put its paw through.

Onga and the princess chatted until the picture began to flicker. Then they said goodbye, the ring faded and the princess disappeared. They heard the cheetah say:

"One day that Onga will go too far!"

The princess said:

"You've got ash all over your paw."

"That's got nothing to do with it," said the cheetah. "And another thing, I don't think that genie of his likes me —"

Then the magic faded completely, and they didn't hear any more.

"You know," said Fearless, when Onga had sailed away, "I really think it's about time I found a beautiful princess and married her."

"Well," said Jasleth, "there's always my sister, Goodness. She's very nice. The thing is, of course, she's still under Maligna's spell at the moment, and she will be until her eighteenth birthday."

"How interesting," said Fearless. "Perhaps I could rescue her or something. It's not a dragon, is it?" he added nervously.

"Oh no," said Jasleth. "Only that business about giving everything to the poor."

"Oh yes, I remember you told me," said Fearless, looking relieved.

So, when Jasleth and Jadelli set out for King Minus' kingdom, Prince Fearless went with them. But before they left, Jasleth went to visit the tiny woman who had helped him, and given him a scarlet cloak when he was going to join the Quest.

"Come in," cried the tiny woman. "How did everything go?"

Jasleth told her all about the adventures they had had, and how they had won the Dragon Hoard, and how he had married the beautiful Princess Jadelli. The tiny woman made him a cup of tea, and also gave him a large plate of iced cakes and some strawberries and cream.

"The point is," said Jasleth, "I'd like to give you something in return for all your kindness to me: some precious pearls, and a gold crown or two, and naturally a Gold stone and a Feast stone and a Luck stone from the Dragon Hoard itself."

"Well," said the tiny woman thoughtfully, "it's very sweet of you, but really, I'd rather not. I'm very happy with my cottage and my squirrels, and looking after the odd traveller that drops by. I don't think I really want a gold crown or pearls. I would like the Feast stone, though, to give to my brother. He has such a job feeding all those people I send to him."

So Jasleth gave her the Feast stone, and a kiss, and went on his way.

Jasleth and Jadelli and Fearless sailed in a nice quiet little ship, and didn't have any adventures, which was probably just as well.

When they got to land, Jasleth went to see the people with the orchard where he had picked apples and hoped for princesses turned into trees. He gave them some presents. They were thrilled, and said any time he wanted to come and talk to their trees in future, he was very welcome. He also found out where the prince lived with his pet two-headed monster. They were playing in the field as usual. Jasleth gave the monster two beautiful pearl necklaces, one for each neck, and it was so pleased it jumped right over an oak tree.

"I never knew you could jump as high as that!" cried its prince happily.

They also went to visit the palace of King August, and Jasleth made sure they all wore their most beautiful clothes. They made King August very uncomfortable by insisting they had come to clean out the cellars and collect the rubbish. King August leaned timidly towards Fearless, and told him they now had a fire-breathing monster that had carried off the princess to do its dusting and sweeping for it, and would Fearless like to rescue her.

But Fearless, who had been told by Jasleth all about the way King August and the princess had behaved last time, said No thank you, it wasn't his week for dragon-slaying. As they went out through the hall, they leaned over the pool and splashed the two dolphins.

It didn't take them long after that to reach King Minus' kingdom.

And there it was, all shining in the evening sunlight, just as Jasleth remembered it, at the back door of the six or seven mountains that were plum-colour at this time of day, not blue.

But when they got closer, alas, what a sorry sight it was. Goodness had made a very thorough job of giving everything away. All the fruit trees were picked bare, and the fields were bare too. The palace was all muddy, with goats running in and out of it, and the beggars' washing all strung up on a line between the pillars. Not far from the palace was a little wooden hut, and outside the hut a girl was sitting on an upturned bucket, looking very sad indeed. She wore a darned, patched grey dress, but her hair was bright golden as a buttercup.

"Whoever is that beautiful girl?" cried Fearless.

"I think," said Jasleth, "it is my sister Goodness."

No sooner had he said this, than Fearless was bounding up to the hut, and humbly bowing, and gallantly asking Goodness what the matter was and if he could help her in any way.

"No," sobbed Goodness. "You see, I've no more presents to give, and no one else to give them to if I had!"

Fearless hastily took out a Gold stone and touched an old iron nail lying on the ground.

"Look," said Fearless. "Here's a golden nail!"

Goodness' face lit up.

"Oh! But who shall I give it to? I know, I'll give it to you. There you are!"

Just then King Minus and the queen and the secretary came out of the hut. They were all dressed in rags, and looked rather thin and fed-up. Princess Goodness' cat looked rather thin and fed-up, as well, and so did Jasleth's chestnut horse, which had refused to stay with the fat beggar Goodness had given it to, and lived in the hut instead.

Jasleth hugged them all, put the Feast stone on their bare table, and produced a wonderful feast with roast chicken and peaches and a honey roll. They had a bit of a job stopping Goodness from running off at once and giving it all to the beggars who were eating far too much as it was. While they were eating, Jasleth explained how he had found his fortune, and how everything was going to be all right. They would want for nothing with a Luck stone to bring them good luck, and a Feast stone to feed them, and a Gold stone to make them rich again. Fearless kept changing bits of metal into gold so Goodness could give them to him. He thought she was a charming girl, and Goodness thought he was charming too, that is, when she wasn't trying to sneak the honey roll out to a goat that appeared in the doorway of the hut.

It didn't take them long to put things right.

After all, they had Jadelli's magic spells to help them as well. The only thing she couldn't do was lift the spell on Goodness. The magic was so strong, she said, that the only way to break it was for Goodness to give her gift to someone else. The snag was that that someone would then keep the gift for always. It seemed better for Goodness to keep it herself until the end of the year, which was now so near, and then lose it altogether.

They built King Minus a brand new palace, all gold with a pearl roof, and let the beggars keep the old one. Jadelli threw some dust over the fruit trees and they all grew fruit, and with the Luck stone sitting in the palace, everyone felt so lucky, they just knew everything was going to be all right. Besides, not only would

Goodness' spell be broken on their eighteenth birthday, but Jasleth would stop turning into a raven, too.

Everyone was happy, except Goodness, who went round all day trying to find people who needed to be given something. Fearless nearly made himself ill stuffing himself with cake and jelly that he pretended he needed to make her feel better.

And then it was the day before Goodness' and Jasleth's eighteenth birthday. Things were back to normal, so the usual sacks of potatoes and crates of ice-cream were piling in, and the little owl, who was not so little any more, was leaning over the edge of the roof, and proudly reading out:

"The card says *HAPPY BIRTHDAY GOODNESS*," when all of a sudden a bat flew down out of the sky and threw a letter rudely in at one of the open palace windows. It was off again, before anybody could ask it what it thought it was doing. King Minus fished the letter out of his porridge and opened it.

Dear Minus, it said, in a nasty scrawly kind of writing. *Thanks to your son Jasleth, I have been buried in my cellar for weeks. Having just got out, and re-built my palace at great personal expense, I notice that today is the dear boy's birthday again, and his sister's too. I shall be over at tea-time without fail. Make sure there are plenty of currants in the birthday cake, and put on some nice hard icing. I don't want my chariot wheels sinking in as they did last time.*

Yours hatefully,
MALIGNA.

King Minus read out the letter and paled.

"It will start all over again," he said. "Only this time she'll think of something worse."

Jasleth changed into a raven, and fell off his chair.

"Except," said Jadelli, "that she's made a mistake. She thinks the birthday is today and not tomorrow."

"I don't see how that can help," said the king.

"I do," said Jadelli.

She got up and went and found Goodness, who was forcing some porridge on a very fat beggar in an ermine cloak.

"I don't want any more," wept the beggar, trying to run away.

"Yes you do," insisted Goodness. "Eat up, you need it!"

"Goodness," said Jadelli kindly, "I know you want to be good, and to help people."

"Oh, yes!" cried Goodness. "But nobody needs anything any more."

"But they do," said Jadelli. "Think how happy everybody would be if they could be as you. What nicer gift could you give anyone than your own gift of goodness?"

Goodness agreed with this wholeheartedly.

"Who can I give it to?" she cried eagerly.

"Well," said Jadelli, "I think you should give it to someone really unhappy. It would cheer her up no end."

Goodness clapped her hands, and immediately went to look for somebody very unhappy, but no one seemed to be. Everyone was getting ready for the birthday, and in high spirits. When they gathered in the hall for tea, Goodness burst into tears.

Just then –

CRASH! BOOM! BANG! *CRASH*!

In through the largest window came a great big
black chariot, with four fed-up-looking, winged
serpents, who couldn't even bother to hiss.

"Ah, ha!" screamed Maligna, and all the bats
flew about in her long black hair.

She was just the same as usual, just as nasty and
bad-tempered, with her nasty, screwed-up, bad-
tempered face.

"Got you!" she yelled, climbing out and pointing
her long white finger at Goodness. "Thought you'd all

got away with it, didn't you?" she added to King Minus, the queen, the secretary, Jasleth, Fearless and Jadelli. "Well!" she shrieked. "This time – "

She got no further.

Goodness, her eyes aglow with delight, ran towards her, and gave Maligna a big hug.

"Poor Maligna!" cried Goodness. "You must be so unhappy, to behave like this! I'll give *you* my gift of goodness. From now on, you'll be as good as I was. No, I don't mind," she said, as Maligna tried to back away. "I *want* you to have it! You *need* it!"

And, of course, it worked, as Jadelli had known it would. In another moment, Maligna's screwed-up features had smoothed out into a most lovely smile.

"Oh!" she cried to the serpents, "you poor darlings! Have some jelly! Please," she begged Goodness, "let me give you this magic mirror – it talks, and it shows you all sorts of places. Listen: *Mirror, mirror, in my hand, who is the fairest in the land?*"

"You are!" said the mirror wearily.

"Me?" gasped Maligna. "Oh, how sweet of you! But of course I'm not, you silly little thing." She gave it a parting kiss, and put it in Goodness' hands.

"I must be getting along!" Maligna added. "I have to give some presents to an old monster on my mountain, and some rabbits too – "

From that day on, Maligna became the nicest, kindest, sweetest enchantress you could hope to meet. Except, of course, whenever you met her, she would insist on giving you things, and they weren't always things you really wanted terribly, although you had to pretend you did so as not to hurt her feelings. Like the gurglebane plant she sent to Jasleth, which grew everywhere, and gurgled at night, so nobody could get any sleep until they had leant out of the window three or four times and told it to shut up.

Still, it was better than being changed into a raven all over the place.

Naturally, after all the excitement was over, Prince Fearless and Princess Goodness got married, and lived happily ever after, the same as Jasleth and Jadelli, and Onga and his princess, and Sillius and Poppy-Lily, and everyone else for that matter. And of course the Luck stones from the Dragon Hoard spread such a lot of luck around, that no one could be unhappy or unlucky again.

Except, that is, for two wolves named Sweetie and Poppet. Maligna was very kind to them nowadays, but they hardly ever got anything to eat – she was always going around feeding the rabbits or visiting the toad's auntie with jellies – and there was never anywhere to sleep as the palace was always full of beggars and poor people. They sat and looked at each other, and they looked down the mountain, too, to see if a nice new postman would come up, and ask them home, but he never did.

"It's no good," said Sweetie. "At this rate we'll starve. We'll just have to go out and find our fortune."

"I suppose," said Poppet, "you're right."

So, in the twilight, they combed each other, and sniffed the air, and hesitated, and growled, and looked back once at the crooked palace.

"Oh, come on," said Poppet.

"I'm coming," said Sweetie.

And they set off.

But you can be sure, if finding a fortune is hard work for a handsome young prince, it's three times harder for a couple of silly, black wolves.

BEAVER BESTSELLERS

You'll find books for everyone to enjoy from Beaver's bestselling range—there are hilarious joke books, gripping reads, wonderful stories, exciting poems and fun activity books. They are available in bookshops or they can be ordered directly from us. Just complete the form below and send the right amount of money and the books will be sent to you at home.

☐ THE ADVENTURES OF KING ROLLO	David McKee	£2.50
☐ MR PINK-WHISTLE STORIES	Enid Blyton	£1.95
☐ FOLK OF THE FARAWAY TREE	Enid Blyton	£1.99
☐ REDWALL	Brian Jacques	£2.95
☐ STRANGERS IN THE HOUSE	Joan Lingard	£1.95
☐ THE RAM OF SWEETRIVER	Colin Dann	£2.50
☐ BAD BOYES	Jim and Duncan Eldridge	£1.95
☐ ANIMAL VERSE	Raymond Wilson	£1.99
☐ A JUMBLE OF JUNGLY JOKES	John Hegarty	£1.50
☐ THE RETURN OF THE ELEPHANT JOKE BOOK	Katie Wales	£1.50
☐ THE REVENGE OF THE BRAIN SHARPENERS	Philip Curtis	£1.50
☐ THE RUNAWAYS	Ruth Thomas	£1.99
☐ EAST OF MIDNIGHT	Tanith Lee	£1.99
☐ THE BARLEY SUGAR GHOST	Hazel Townson	£1.50
☐ CRAZY COOKING	Juliet Bawden	£2.25

If you would like to order books, please send this form, and the money due to:

ARROW BOOKS, BOOKSERVICE BY POST, PO BOX 29, DOUGLAS, ISLE OF MAN, BRITISH ISLES. Please enclose a cheque or postal order made out to Arrow Books Ltd for the amount due including 22p per book for postage and packing both for orders within the UK and for overseas orders.

NAME ....

ADDRESS ....

....

Please print clearly.

Whilst every effort is made to keep prices low it is sometimes necessary to increase cover prices at short notice. Arrow Books reserve the right to show new retail prices on covers which may differ from those previously advertised in the text or elsewhere.

BEAVER BOOKS FOR OLDER READERS

There are loads of exciting books for older readers in Beaver. They are available in bookshops or they can be ordered directly from us. Just complete the form below and send the right amount of money and the books will be sent to you at home.

☐	THE RUNAWAYS	Ruth Thomas	£1.99
☐	COMPANIONS ON THE ROAD	Tanith Lee	£1.99
☐	THE GOOSEBERRY	Joan Lingard	£1.95
☐	IN THE GRIP OF WINTER	Colin Dann	£2.50
☐	THE TEMPEST TWINS Books 1 – 6	John Harvey	£1.99
☐	YOUR FRIEND, REBECCA	Linda Hoy	£1.99
☐	THE TIME OF THE GHOST	Diana Wynne Jones	£1.95
☐	WATER LANE	Tom Aitken	£1.95
☐	ALANNA	Tamora Pierce	£2.50
☐	REDWALL	Brian Jacques	£2.95
☐	BUT JASPER CAME INSTEAD	Christine Nostlinger	£1.95
☐	A BOTTLED CHERRY ANGEL	Jean Ure	£1.99
☐	A HAWK IN SILVER	Mary Gentle	£1.99
☐	WHITE FANG	Jack London	£1.95
☐	FANGS OF THE WEREWOLF	John Halkin	£1.95

If you would like to order books, please send this form, and the money due to:
ARROW BOOKS, BOOKSERVICE BY POST, PO BOX 29, DOUGLAS, ISLE OF MAN, BRITISH ISLES. Please enclose a cheque or postal order made out to Arrow Books Ltd for the amount due including 22p per book for postage and packing both for orders within the UK and for overseas orders.

NAME ....

ADDRESS ....

....

Please print clearly.

Whilst every effort is made to keep prices low it is sometimes necessary to increase cover prices at short notice. Arrow Books reserve the right to show new retail prices on covers which may differ from those previously advertised in the text or elsewhere.

JOAN LINGARD

If you enjoyed this book, perhaps you ought to try some more of our Joan Lingard titles. They are available in bookshops or they can be ordered directly from us. Just complete the form below and enclose the right amount of money and the books will be sent to you at home.

☐	Maggie 1: The Clearance	£1.95
☐	Maggie 2: The Resettling	£1.95
☐	Maggie 3: The Pilgrimage	£1.95
☐	Maggie 4: The Reunion	£1.95
☐	The File on Fraulein Berg	£1.50
☐	The Winter Visitor	£1.25
☐	Strangers in the House	£1.95
☐	The Gooseberry	£1.95

If you would like to order books, please send this form, and the money due to:

ARROW BOOKS, BOOKSERVICE BY POST, PO BOX 29, DOUGLAS, ISLE OF MAN, BRITISH ISLES. Please enclose a cheque or postal order made out to Arrow Books Ltd for the amount due including 30p per book for postage and packing both for orders within the UK and for overseas orders.

NAME ....

ADDRESS ....

....

Please print clearly.